A LUCKY LUKE ADVENTURE

THE DALTONS' STASH

ARTWORK BY MORRIS
SCRIPT BY MORRIS WITH THE HELP OF VICQ

 9th CINEBOOK
The 9th Art Publisher

Original title: Le Magot Des Dalton
Original edition: © Dargaud Editeur Paris 1980 by Morris and Vicq
© Lucky Comics, 2016
www.lucky-luke.com
English translation: © 2016 Cinebook Ltd
Translator: Jerome Saincantin
Lettering and text layout: Design Amorandi
Printed in Spain by EGEDSA
This edition first published in Great Britain in 2016 by
Cinebook Ltd
56 Beech Avenue
Canterbury, Kent
CT4 7TA
www.cinebook.com
A CIP catalogue record for this book
is available from the British Library
ISBN 978-1-84918-298-0

9th CINEBOOK
The 9th Art Publisher

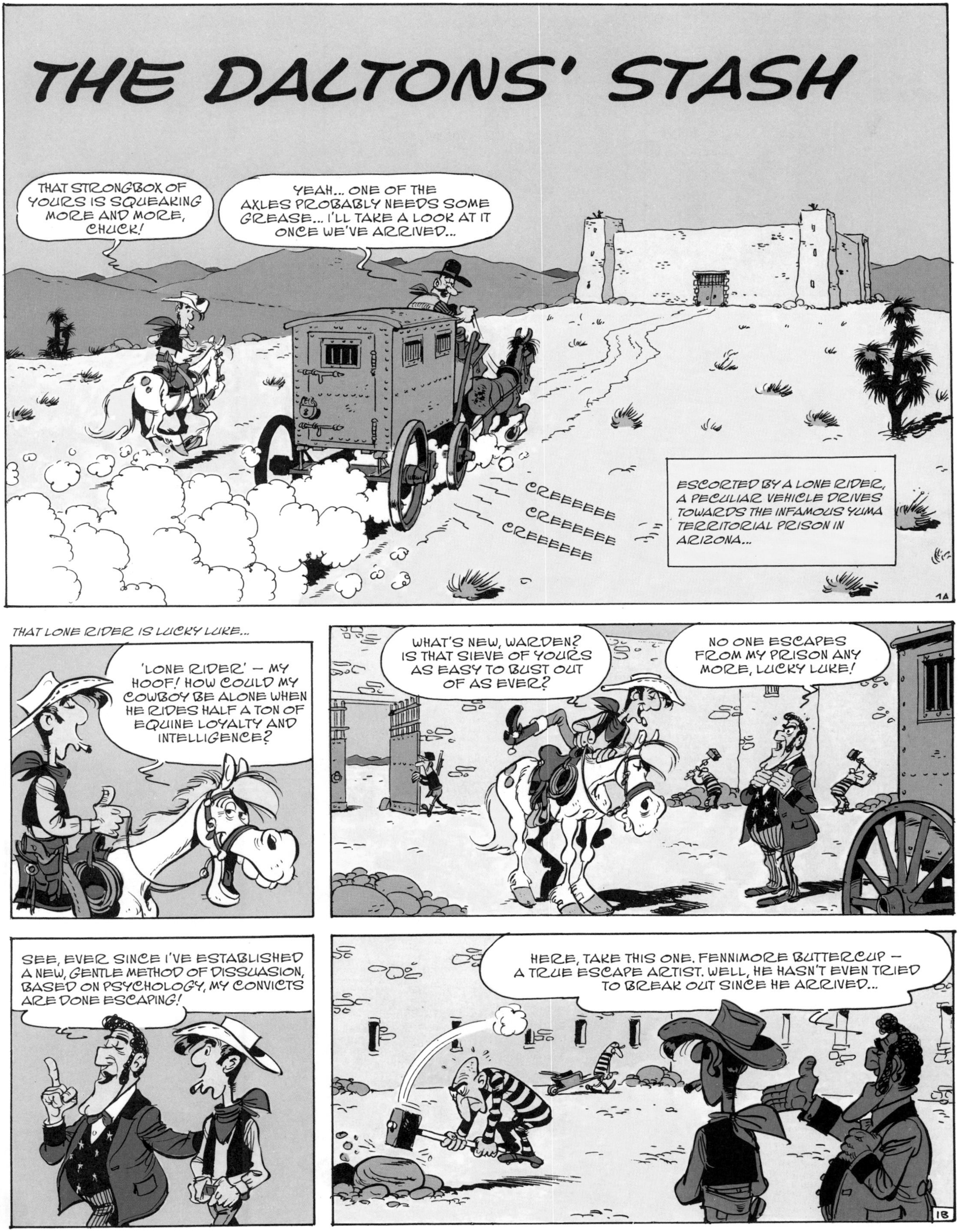
THE DALTONS' STASH
THAT STRONGBOX OF YOURS IS SQUEAKING MORE AND MORE, CHUCK!
YEAH... ONE OF THE AXLES PROBABLY NEEDS SOME GREASE... I'LL TAKE A LOOK AT IT ONCE WE'VE ARRIVED...
CREEEEEEE
CREEEEEEE
CREEEEEEE
ESCORTED BY A LONE RIDER, A PECULIAR VEHICLE DRIVES TOWARDS THE INFAMOUS YUMA TERRITORIAL PRISON IN ARIZONA...
1A
THAT LONE RIDER IS LUCKY LUKE...
'LONE RIDER' – MY HOOF! HOW COULD MY COWBOY BE ALONE WHEN HE RIDES HALF A TON OF EQUINE LOYALTY AND INTELLIGENCE?
WHAT'S NEW, WARDEN? IS THAT SIEVE OF YOURS AS EASY TO BUST OUT OF AS EVER?
NO ONE ESCAPES FROM MY PRISON ANY MORE, LUCKY LUKE!
SEE, EVER SINCE I'VE ESTABLISHED A NEW, GENTLE METHOD OF DISSUASION, BASED ON PSYCHOLOGY, MY CONVICTS ARE DONE ESCAPING!
HERE, TAKE THIS ONE. FENNIMORE BUTTERCUP – A TRUE ESCAPE ARTIST. WELL, HE HASN'T EVEN TRIED TO BREAK OUT SINCE HE ARRIVED...
1B

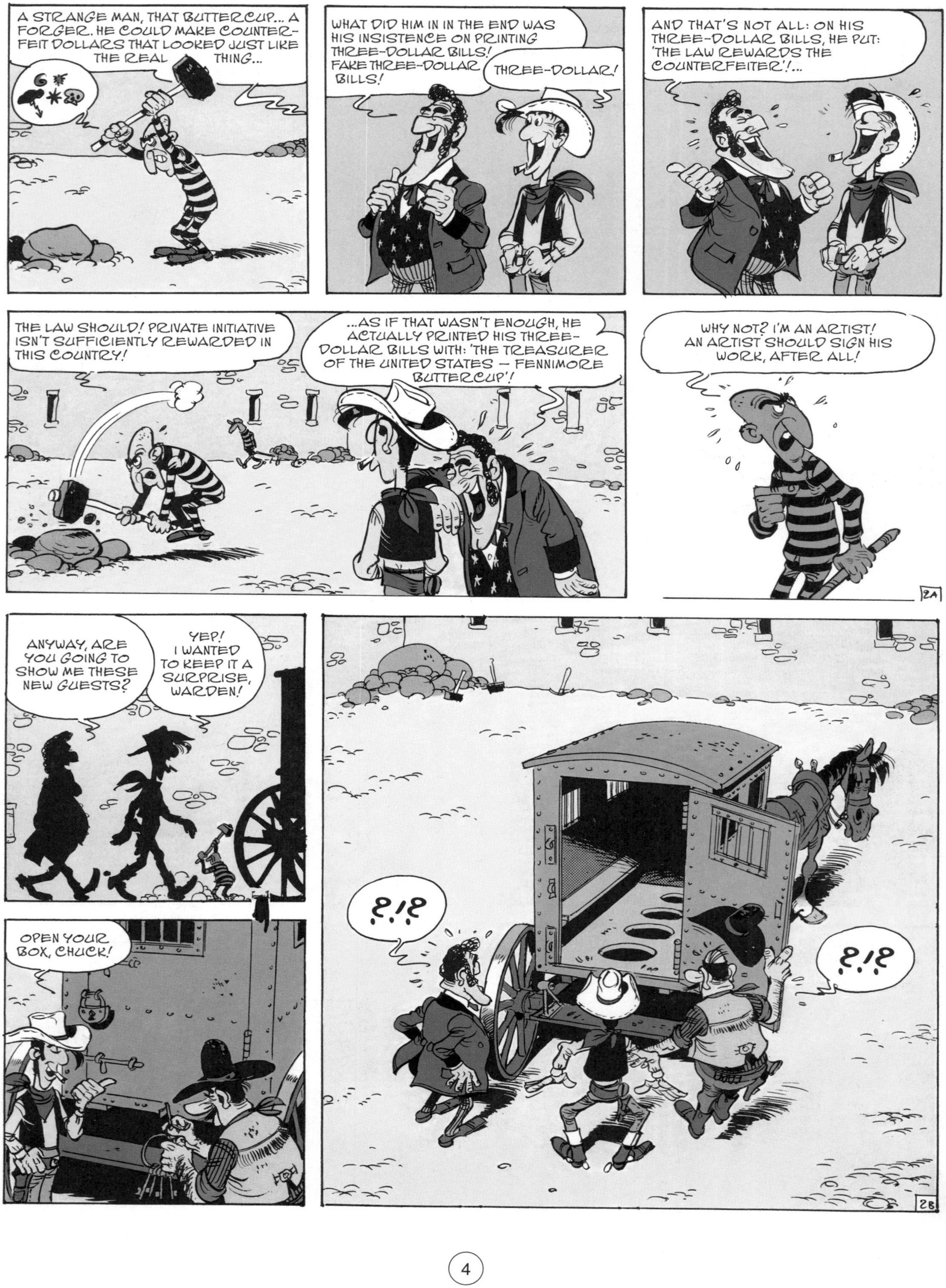

A STRANGE MAN, THAT BUTTERCUP... A FORGER. HE COULD MAKE COUNTERFEIT DOLLARS THAT LOOKED JUST LIKE THE REAL THING...
WHAT DID HIM IN IN THE END WAS HIS INSISTENCE ON PRINTING THREE-DOLLAR BILLS! FAKE THREE-DOLLAR BILLS!
THREE-DOLLAR!
AND THAT'S NOT ALL: ON HIS THREE-DOLLAR BILLS, HE PUT: 'THE LAW REWARDS THE COUNTERFEITER'!...
THE LAW SHOULD! PRIVATE INITIATIVE ISN'T SUFFICIENTLY REWARDED IN THIS COUNTRY!
...AS IF THAT WASN'T ENOUGH, HE ACTUALLY PRINTED HIS THREE-DOLLAR BILLS WITH: 'THE TREASURER OF THE UNITED STATES – FENNIMORE BUTTERCUP'!
WHY NOT? I'M AN ARTIST! AN ARTIST SHOULD SIGN HIS WORK, AFTER ALL!
2A
ANYWAY, ARE YOU GOING TO SHOW ME THESE NEW GUESTS?
YEP! I WANTED TO KEEP IT A SURPRISE, WARDEN!
OPEN YOUR BOX, CHUCK!
?!?
?!?
2B

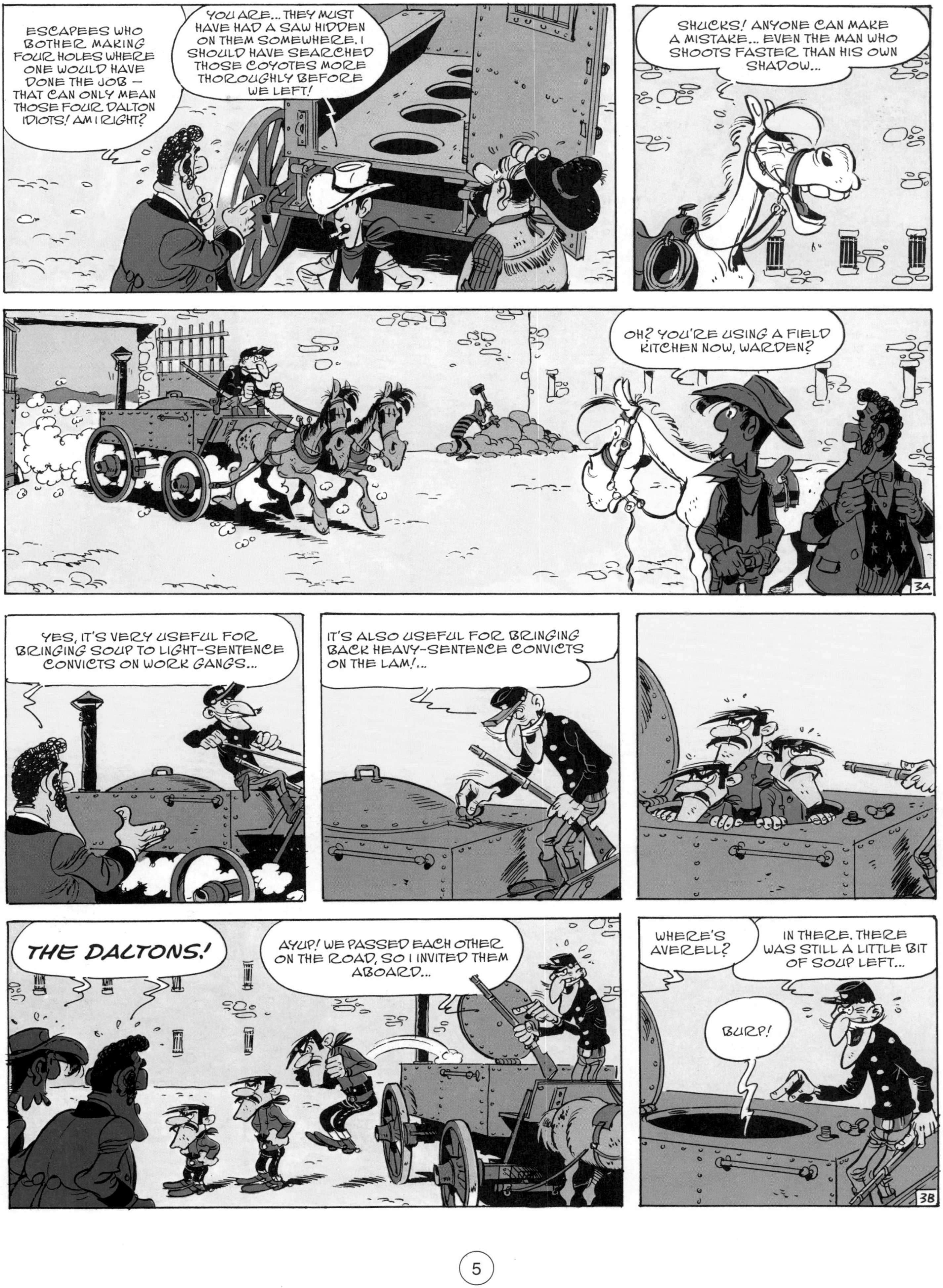

ESCAPEES WHO BOTHER MAKING FOUR HOLES WHERE ONE WOULD HAVE DONE THE JOB – THAT CAN ONLY MEAN THOSE FOUR DALTON IDIOTS! AM I RIGHT?
YOU ARE... THEY MUST HAVE HAD A SAW HIDDEN ON THEM SOMEWHERE. I SHOULD HAVE SEARCHED THOSE COYOTES MORE THOROUGHLY BEFORE WE LEFT!
SHUCKS! ANYONE CAN MAKE A MISTAKE... EVEN THE MAN WHO SHOOTS FASTER THAN HIS OWN SHADOW...
OH? YOU'RE USING A FIELD KITCHEN NOW, WARDEN?
3A
YES, IT'S VERY USEFUL FOR BRINGING SOUP TO LIGHT-SENTENCE CONVICTS ON WORK GANGS...
IT'S ALSO USEFUL FOR BRINGING BACK HEAVY-SENTENCE CONVICTS ON THE LAM!...
THE DALTONS!
AYUP! WE PASSED EACH OTHER ON THE ROAD, SO I INVITED THEM ABOARD...
WHERE'S AVERELL?
IN THERE. THERE WAS STILL A LITTLE BIT OF SOUP LEFT...
BURP!
3B

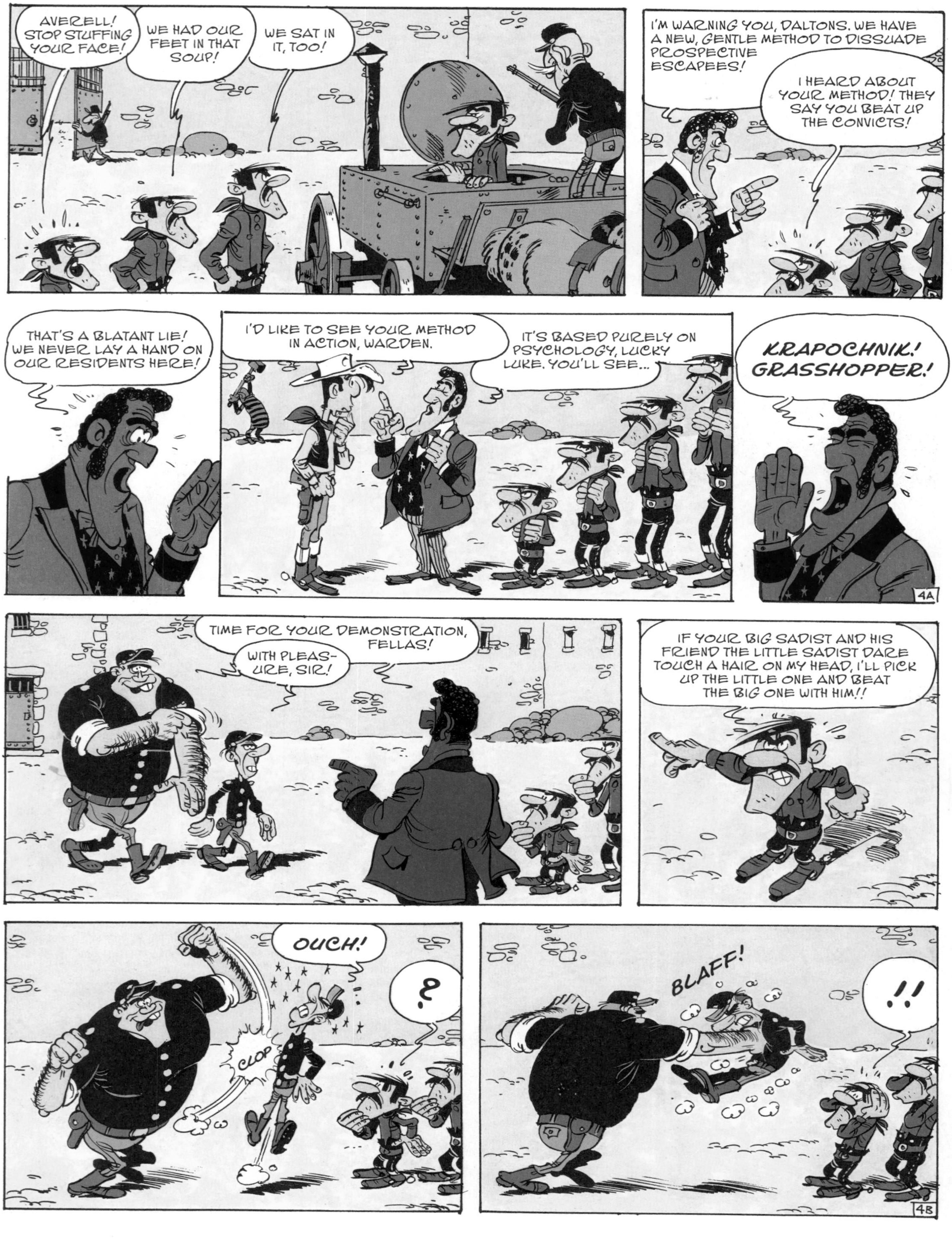
AVERELL! STOP STUFFING YOUR FACE!
WE HAD OUR FEET IN THAT SOUP!
WE SAT IN IT, TOO!
I'M WARNING YOU, DALTONS. WE HAVE A NEW, GENTLE METHOD TO DISSUADE PROSPECTIVE ESCAPEES!
I HEARD ABOUT YOUR METHOD! THEY SAY YOU BEAT UP THE CONVICTS!
THAT'S A BLATANT LIE! WE NEVER LAY A HAND ON OUR RESIDENTS HERE!
I'D LIKE TO SEE YOUR METHOD IN ACTION, WARDEN.
IT'S BASED PURELY ON PSYCHOLOGY, LUCKY LUKE. YOU'LL SEE...
KRAPOCHNIK! GRASSHOPPER!
4A
TIME FOR YOUR DEMONSTRATION, FELLAS!
WITH PLEAS-URE, SIR!
IF YOUR BIG SADIST AND HIS FRIEND THE LITTLE SADIST DARE TOUCH A HAIR ON MY HEAD, I'LL PICK UP THE LITTLE ONE AND BEAT THE BIG ONE WITH HIM!!
OUCH!
CLOP
?
BLAFF!
!!
4B

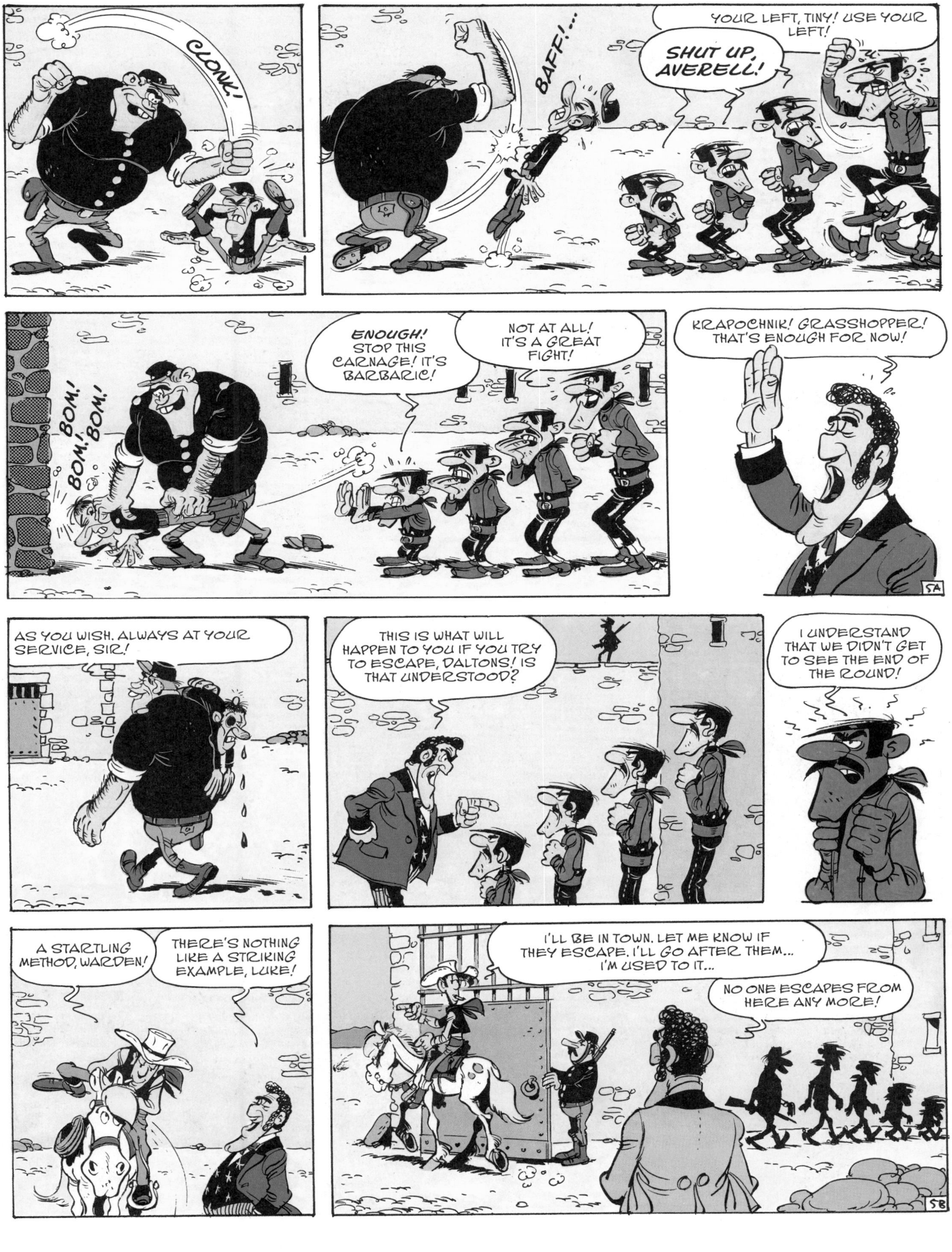
CLONK!
BAFF!...
YOUR LEFT, TINY! USE YOUR LEFT!
SHUT UP, AVERELL!
BOM! BOM! BOM!
ENOUGH! STOP THIS CARNAGE! IT'S BARBARIC!
NOT AT ALL! IT'S A GREAT FIGHT!
KRAPOCHNIK! GRASSHOPPER! THAT'S ENOUGH FOR NOW!
AS YOU WISH. ALWAYS AT YOUR SERVICE, SIR!
THIS IS WHAT WILL HAPPEN TO YOU IF YOU TRY TO ESCAPE, DALTONS! IS THAT UNDERSTOOD?
I UNDERSTAND THAT WE DIDN'T GET TO SEE THE END OF THE ROUND!
A STARTLING METHOD, WARDEN!
THERE'S NOTHING LIKE A STRIKING EXAMPLE, LUKE!
I'LL BE IN TOWN. LET ME KNOW IF THEY ESCAPE. I'LL GO AFTER THEM... I'M USED TO IT...
NO ONE ESCAPES FROM HERE ANY MORE!

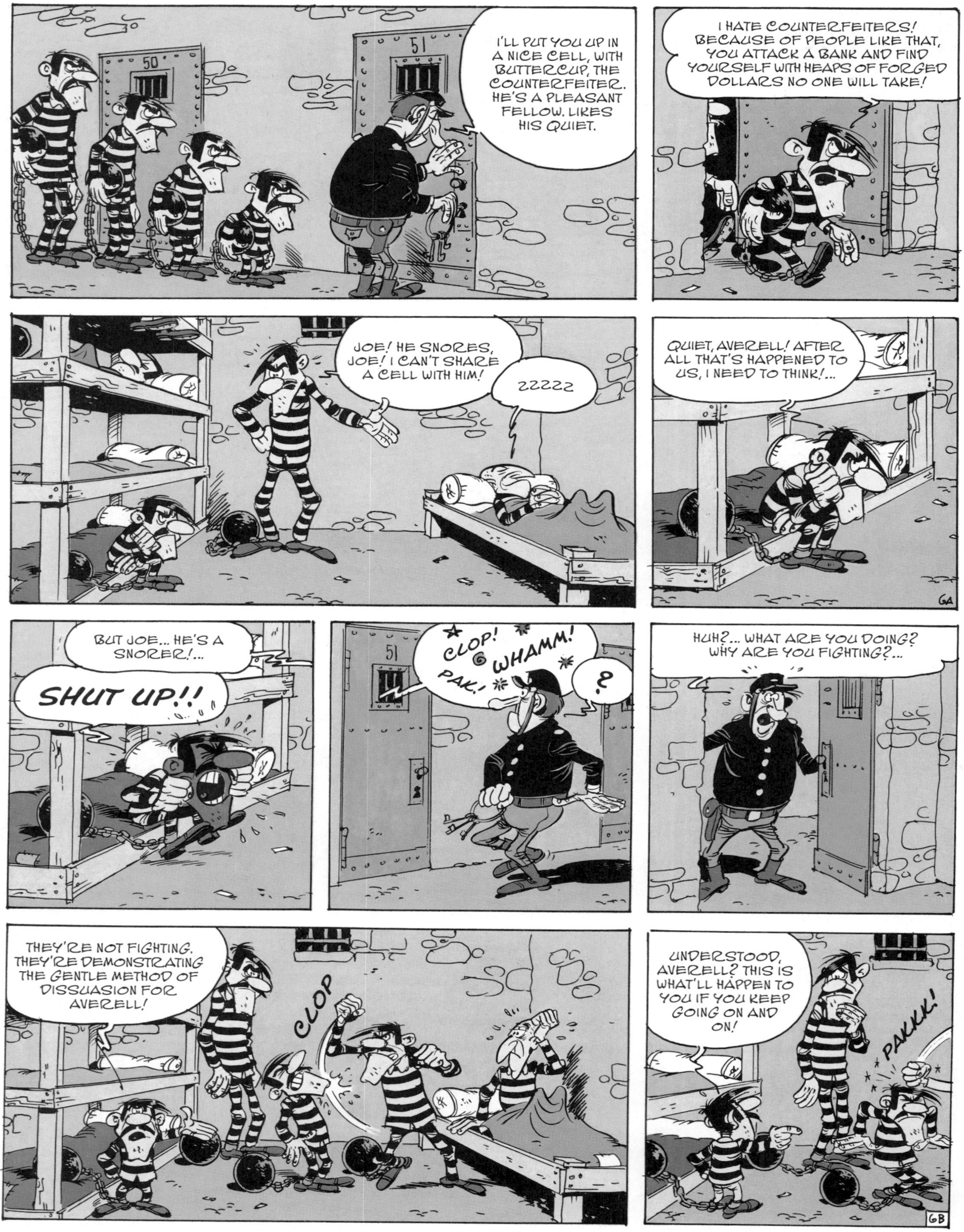
I'LL PUT YOU UP IN A NICE CELL, WITH BUTTERCUP, THE COUNTERFEITER. HE'S A PLEASANT FELLOW. LIKES HIS QUIET.
I HATE COUNTERFEITERS! BECAUSE OF PEOPLE LIKE THAT, YOU ATTACK A BANK AND FIND YOURSELF WITH HEAPS OF FORGED DOLLARS NO ONE WILL TAKE!
JOE! HE SNORES, JOE! I CAN'T SHARE A CELL WITH HIM!
ZZZZZ
QUIET, AVERELL! AFTER ALL THAT'S HAPPENED TO US, I NEED TO THINK!...
BUT JOE... HE'S A SNORER!...
SHUT UP!!
CLOP! WHAMM! PAK!
?
HUH?... WHAT ARE YOU DOING? WHY ARE YOU FIGHTING?...
THEY'RE NOT FIGHTING. THEY'RE DEMONSTRATING THE GENTLE METHOD OF DISSUASION FOR AVERELL!
CLOP
UNDERSTOOD, AVERELL? THIS IS WHAT'LL HAPPEN TO YOU IF YOU KEEP GOING ON AND ON!
PAKKK!

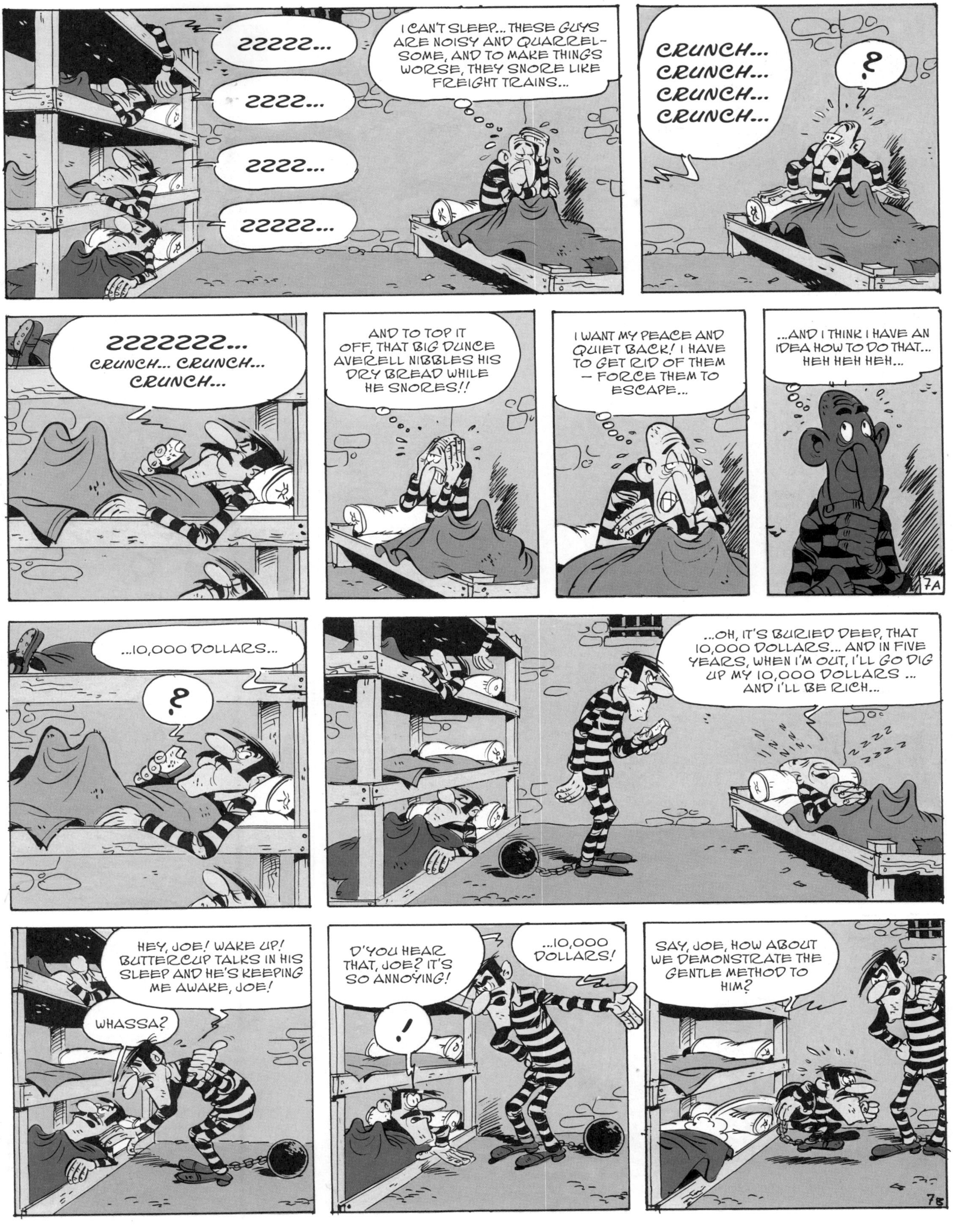

ZZZZZ...
ZZZZ...
ZZZZ...
ZZZZZ...
I CAN'T SLEEP... THESE GUYS ARE NOISY AND QUARREL-SOME, AND TO MAKE THINGS WORSE, THEY SNORE LIKE FREIGHT TRAINS...
CRUNCH... CRUNCH... CRUNCH... CRUNCH...
?
ZZZZZZZ... CRUNCH... CRUNCH... CRUNCH...
AND TO TOP IT OFF, THAT BIG DUNCE AVERELL NIBBLES HIS DRY BREAD WHILE HE SNORES!!
I WANT MY PEACE AND QUIET BACK! I HAVE TO GET RID OF THEM – FORCE THEM TO ESCAPE...
...AND I THINK I HAVE AN IDEA HOW TO DO THAT... HEH HEH HEH...
7A
...10,000 DOLLARS...
?
...OH, IT'S BURIED DEEP, THAT 10,000 DOLLARS... AND IN FIVE YEARS, WHEN I'M OUT, I'LL GO DIG UP MY 10,000 DOLLARS ... AND I'LL BE RICH...
HEY, JOE! WAKE UP! BUTTERCUP TALKS IN HIS SLEEP AND HE'S KEEPING ME AWAKE, JOE!
WHASSA?
D'YOU HEAR THAT, JOE? IT'S SO ANNOYING!
!
...10,000 DOLLARS!
SAY, JOE, HOW ABOUT WE DEMONSTRATE THE GENTLE METHOD TO HIM?
7B

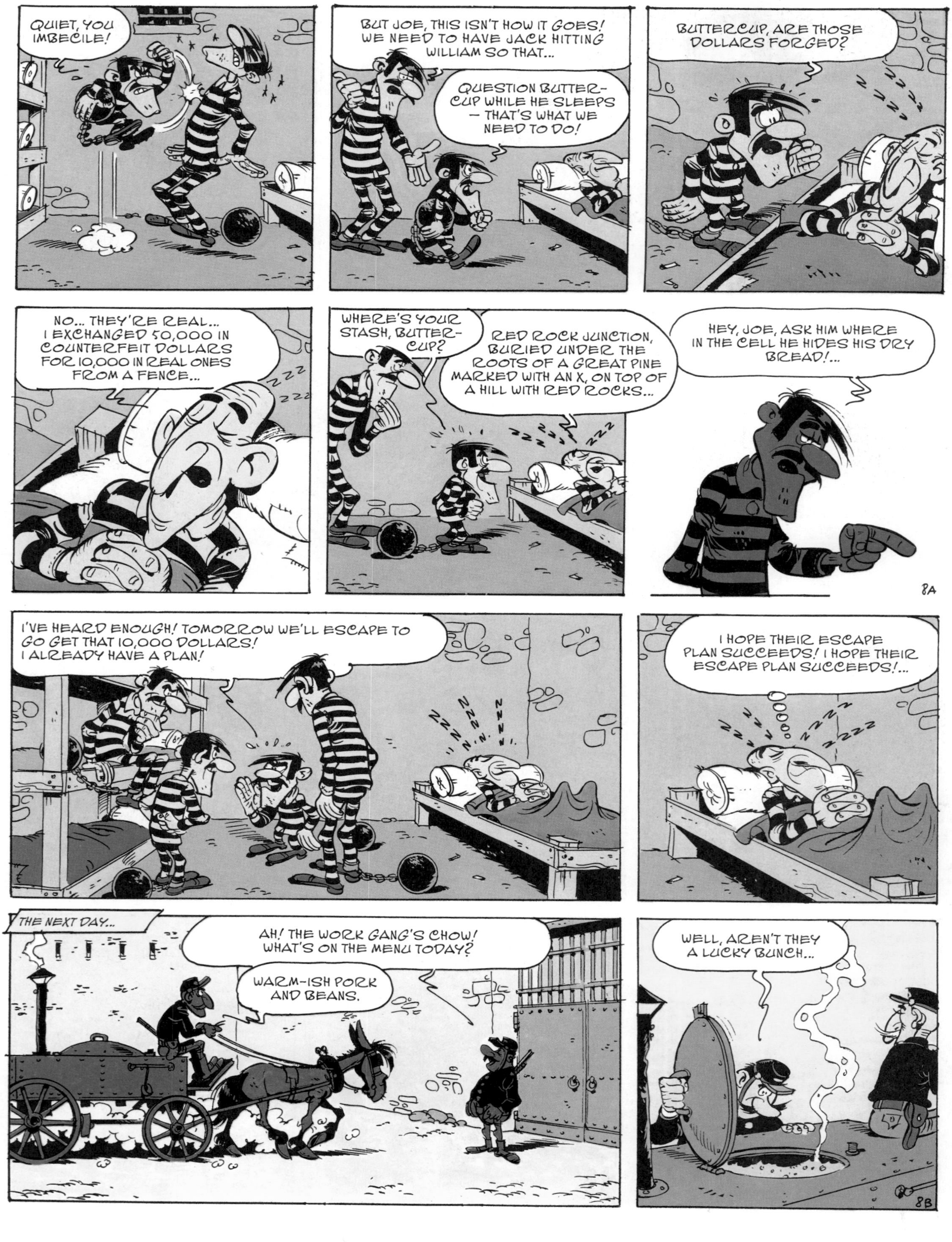
QUIET, YOU IMBECILE!
BUT JOE, THIS ISN'T HOW IT GOES! WE NEED TO HAVE JACK HITTING WILLIAM SO THAT...
QUESTION BUTTERCUP WHILE HE SLEEPS – THAT'S WHAT WE NEED TO DO!
BUTTERCUP, ARE THOSE DOLLARS FORGED?
NO... THEY'RE REAL... I EXCHANGED 50,000 IN COUNTERFEIT DOLLARS FOR 10,000 IN REAL ONES FROM A FENCE...
WHERE'S YOUR STASH, BUTTERCUP?
RED ROCK JUNCTION, BURIED UNDER THE ROOTS OF A GREAT PINE MARKED WITH AN X, ON TOP OF A HILL WITH RED ROCKS...
HEY, JOE, ASK HIM WHERE IN THE CELL HE HIDES HIS DRY BREAD!...
8A
I'VE HEARD ENOUGH! TOMORROW WE'LL ESCAPE TO GO GET THAT 10,000 DOLLARS! I ALREADY HAVE A PLAN!
I HOPE THEIR ESCAPE PLAN SUCCEEDS! I HOPE THEIR ESCAPE PLAN SUCCEEDS!...
THE NEXT DAY...
AH! THE WORK GANG'S CHOW! WHAT'S ON THE MENU TODAY?
WARM-ISH PORK AND BEANS.
WELL, AREN'T THEY A LUCKY BUNCH...
8B

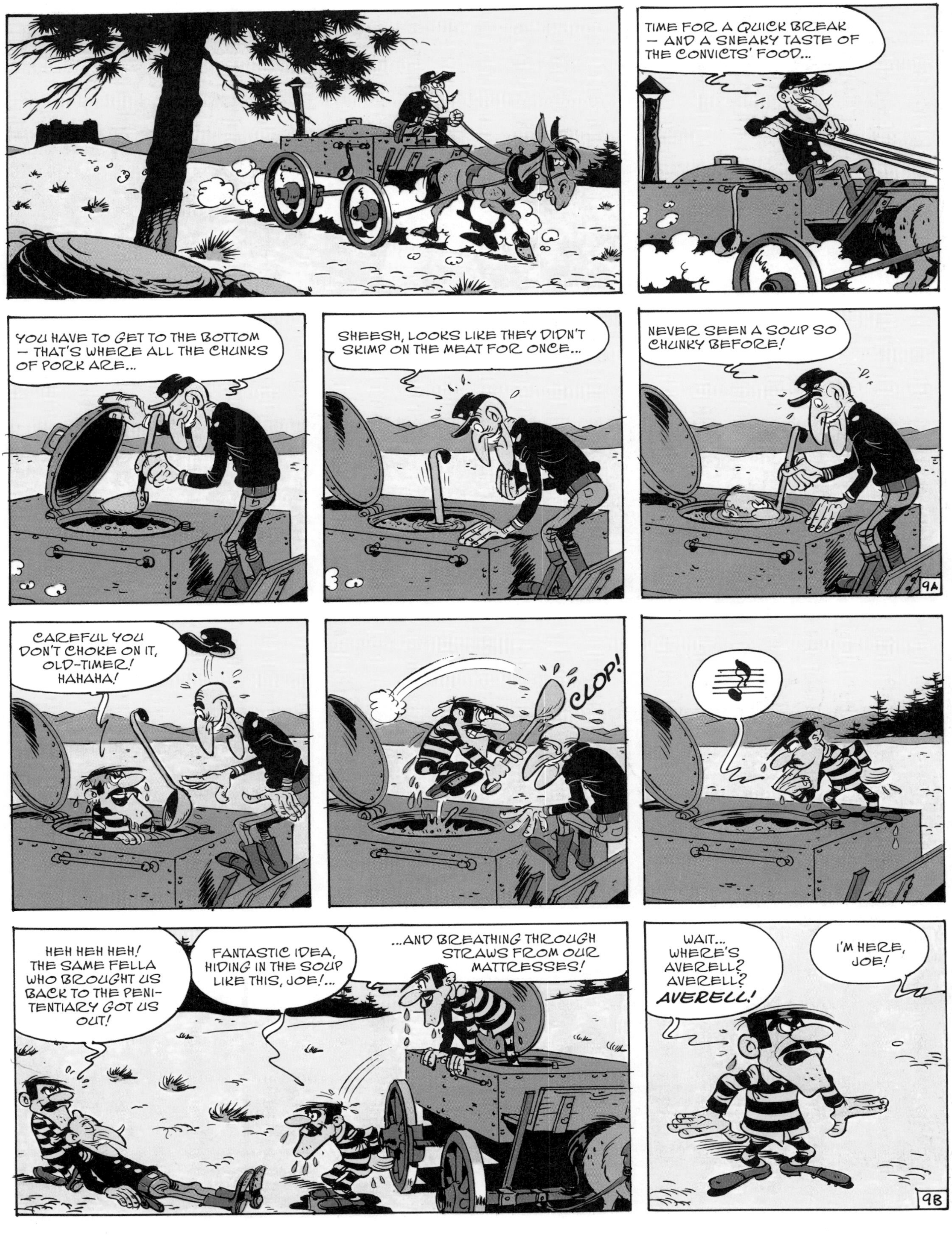
TIME FOR A QUICK BREAK — AND A SNEAKY TASTE OF THE CONVICTS' FOOD...
YOU HAVE TO GET TO THE BOTTOM — THAT'S WHERE ALL THE CHUNKS OF PORK ARE...
SHEESH, LOOKS LIKE THEY DIDN'T SKIMP ON THE MEAT FOR ONCE...
NEVER SEEN A SOUP SO CHUNKY BEFORE!
9A
CAREFUL YOU DON'T CHOKE ON IT, OLD-TIMER! HAHAHA!
CLOP!
HEH HEH HEH! THE SAME FELLA WHO BROUGHT US BACK TO THE PENITENTIARY GOT US OUT!
FANTASTIC IDEA, HIDING IN THE SOUP LIKE THIS, JOE!...
...AND BREATHING THROUGH STRAWS FROM OUR MATTRESSES!
WAIT... WHERE'S AVERELL? AVERELL? AVERELL!
I'M HERE, JOE!
9B

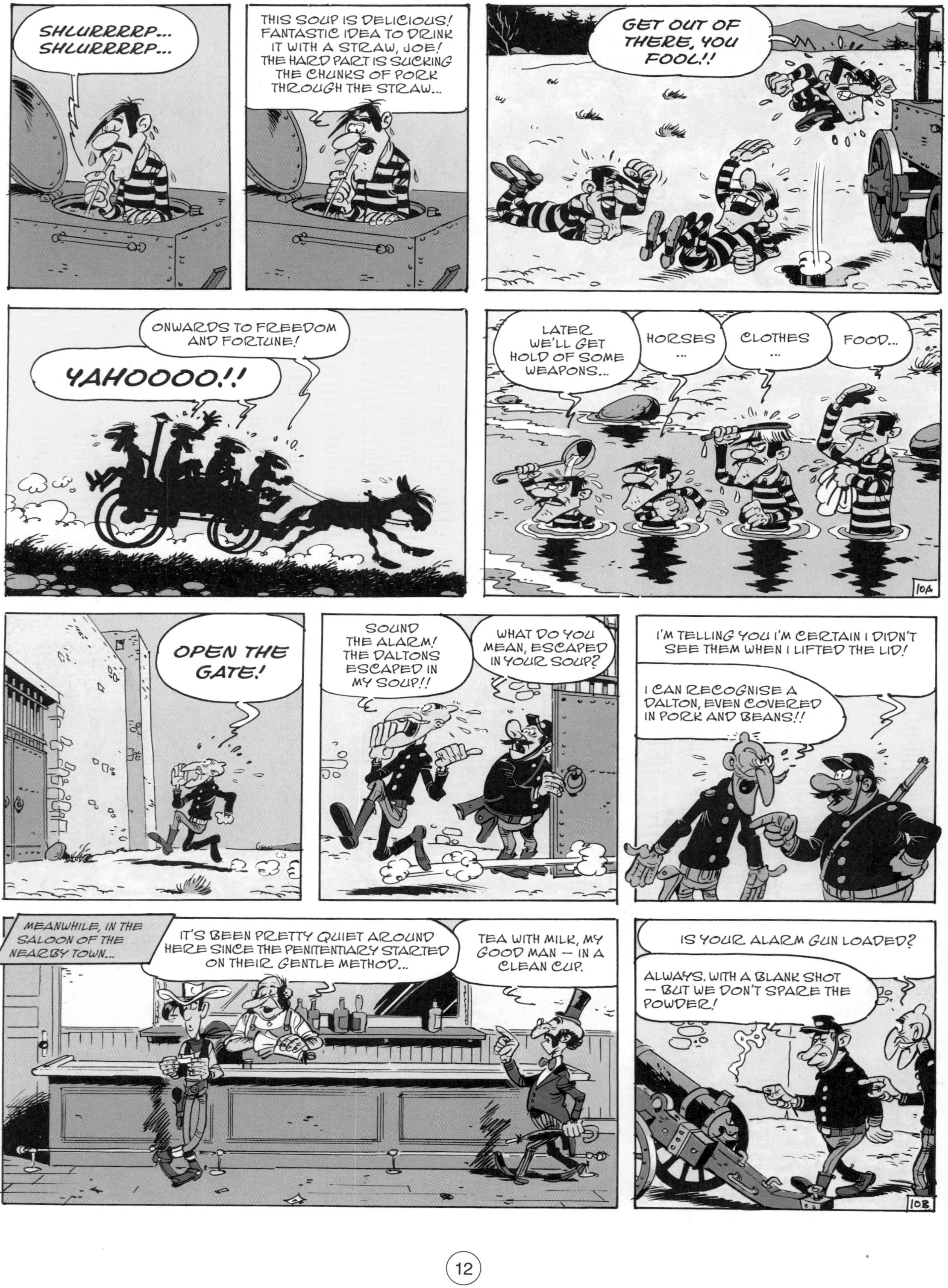

SHLURRRRP... SHLURRRRP...
THIS SOUP IS DELICIOUS! FANTASTIC IDEA TO DRINK IT WITH A STRAW, JOE! THE HARD PART IS SUCKING THE CHUNKS OF PORK THROUGH THE STRAW...
GET OUT OF THERE, YOU FOOL!!
ONWARDS TO FREEDOM AND FORTUNE!
YAHOOOO!!
LATER WE'LL GET HOLD OF SOME WEAPONS...
HORSES ...
CLOTHES ...
FOOD...
10A
OPEN THE GATE!
SOUND THE ALARM! THE DALTONS ESCAPED IN MY SOUP!!
WHAT DO YOU MEAN, ESCAPED IN YOUR SOUP?
I'M TELLING YOU I'M CERTAIN I DIDN'T SEE THEM WHEN I LIFTED THE LID!
I CAN RECOGNISE A DALTON, EVEN COVERED IN PORK AND BEANS!!
MEANWHILE, IN THE SALOON OF THE NEARBY TOWN...
IT'S BEEN PRETTY QUIET AROUND HERE SINCE THE PENITENTIARY STARTED ON THEIR GENTLE METHOD...
TEA WITH MILK, MY GOOD MAN — IN A CLEAN CUP.
IS YOUR ALARM GUN LOADED?
ALWAYS. WITH A BLANK SHOT — BUT WE DON'T SPARE THE POWDER!
10B

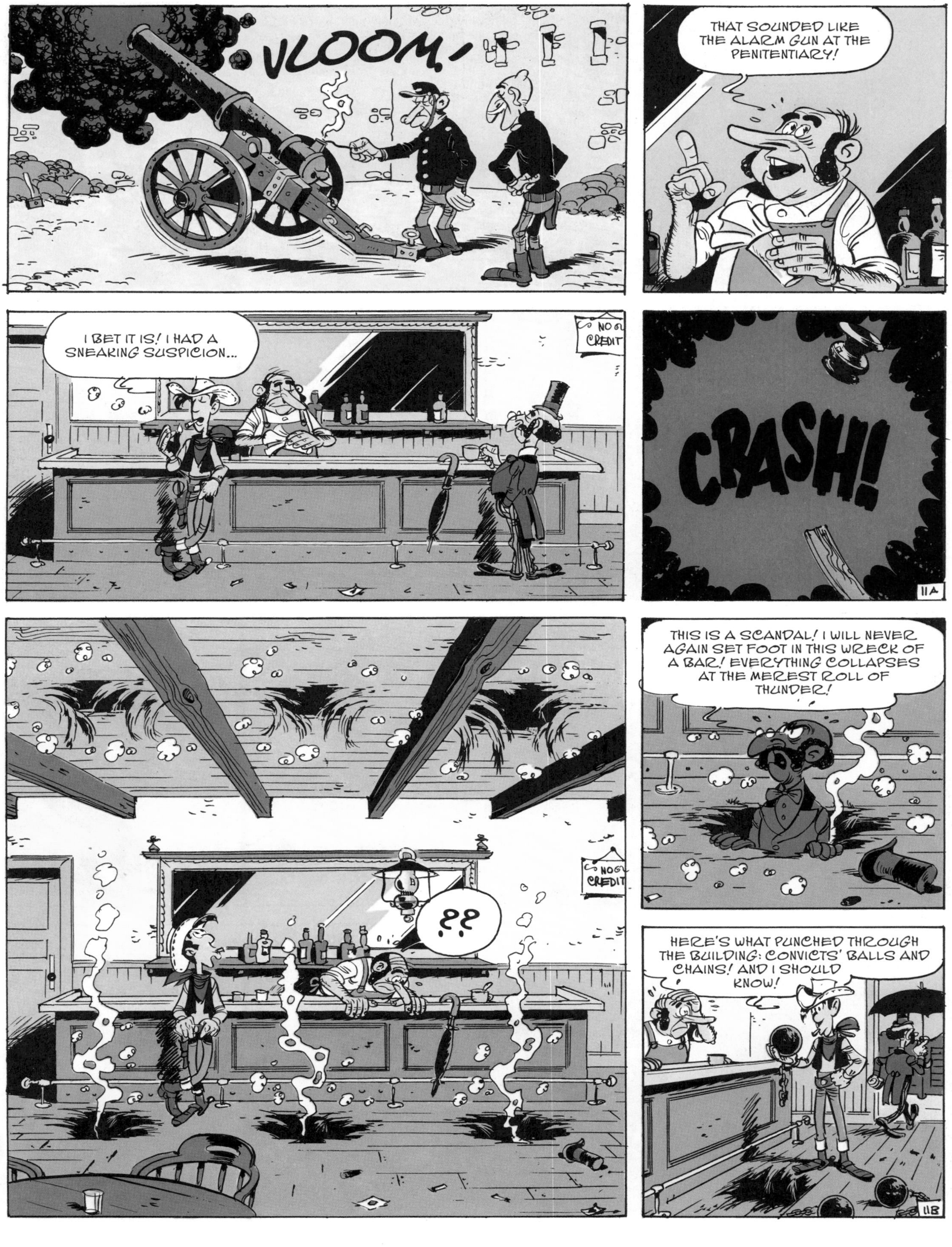
VLOOM!
THAT SOUNDED LIKE THE ALARM GUN AT THE PENITENTIARY!
I BET IT IS! I HAD A SNEAKING SUSPICION...
NO CREDIT
CRASH!
11A
??
NO CREDIT
THIS IS A SCANDAL! I WILL NEVER AGAIN SET FOOT IN THIS WRECK OF A BAR! EVERYTHING COLLAPSES AT THE MEREST ROLL OF THUNDER!
HERE'S WHAT PUNCHED THROUGH THE BUILDING: CONVICTS' BALLS AND CHAINS! AND I SHOULD KNOW!
11B

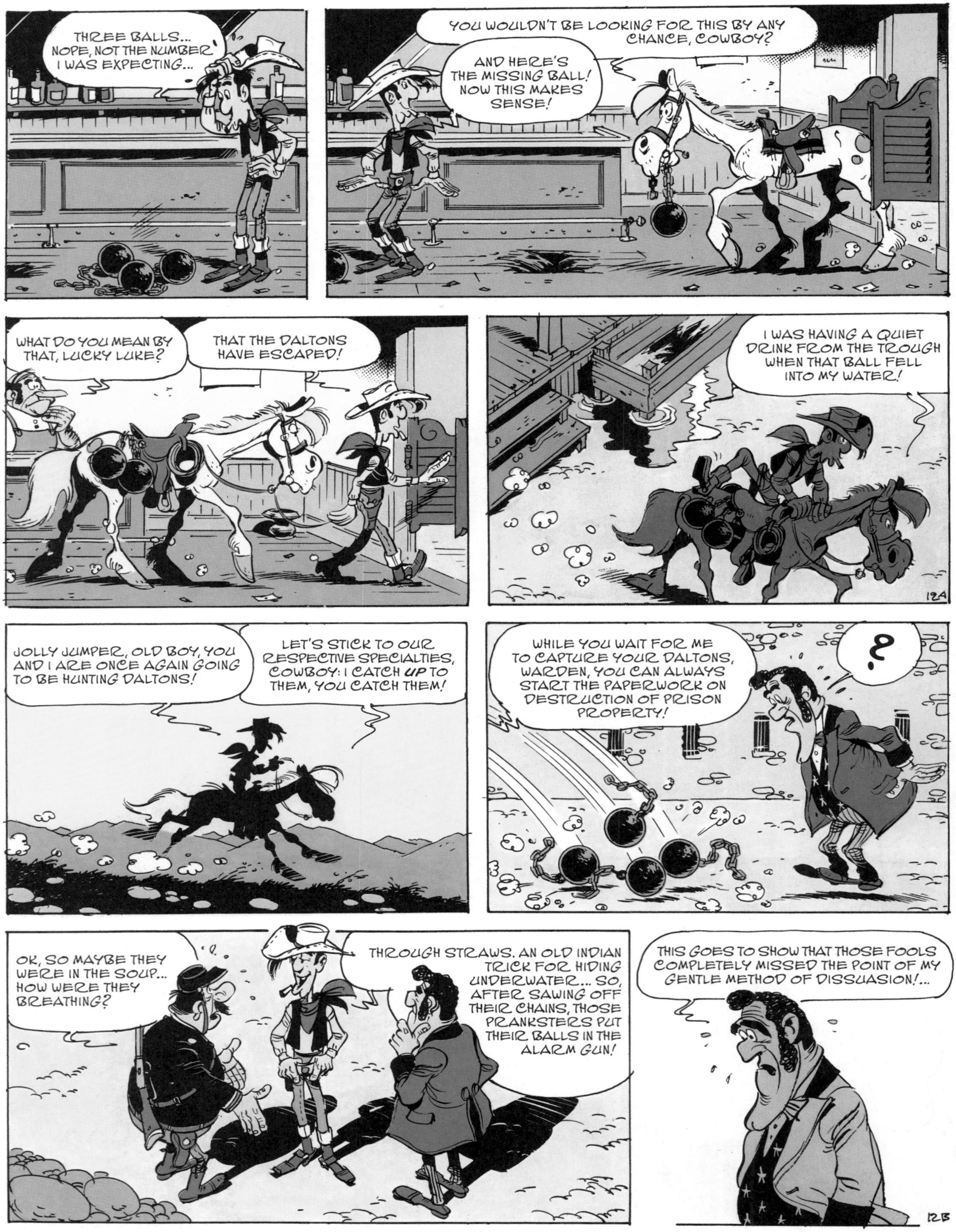
THREE BALLS... NOPE, NOT THE NUMBER I WAS EXPECTING...
YOU WOULDN'T BE LOOKING FOR THIS BY ANY CHANCE, COWBOY?
AND HERE'S THE MISSING BALL! NOW THIS MAKES SENSE!
WHAT DO YOU MEAN BY THAT, LUCKY LUKE?
THAT THE DALTONS HAVE ESCAPED!
I WAS HAVING A QUIET DRINK FROM THE TROUGH WHEN THAT BALL FELL INTO MY WATER!
12A
JOLLY JUMPER, OLD BOY, YOU AND I ARE ONCE AGAIN GOING TO BE HUNTING DALTONS!
LET'S STICK TO OUR RESPECTIVE SPECIALTIES, COWBOY: I CATCH UP TO THEM, YOU CATCH THEM!
WHILE YOU WAIT FOR ME TO CAPTURE YOUR DALTONS, WARDEN, YOU CAN ALWAYS START THE PAPERWORK ON DESTRUCTION OF PRISON PROPERTY!
?
OK, SO MAYBE THEY WERE IN THE SOUP... HOW WERE THEY BREATHING?
THROUGH STRAWS. AN OLD INDIAN TRICK FOR HIDING UNDERWATER... SO, AFTER SAWING OFF THEIR CHAINS, THOSE PRANKSTERS PUT THEIR BALLS IN THE ALARM GUN!
THIS GOES TO SHOW THAT THOSE FOOLS COMPLETELY MISSED THE POINT OF MY GENTLE METHOD OF DISSUASION!...
12B

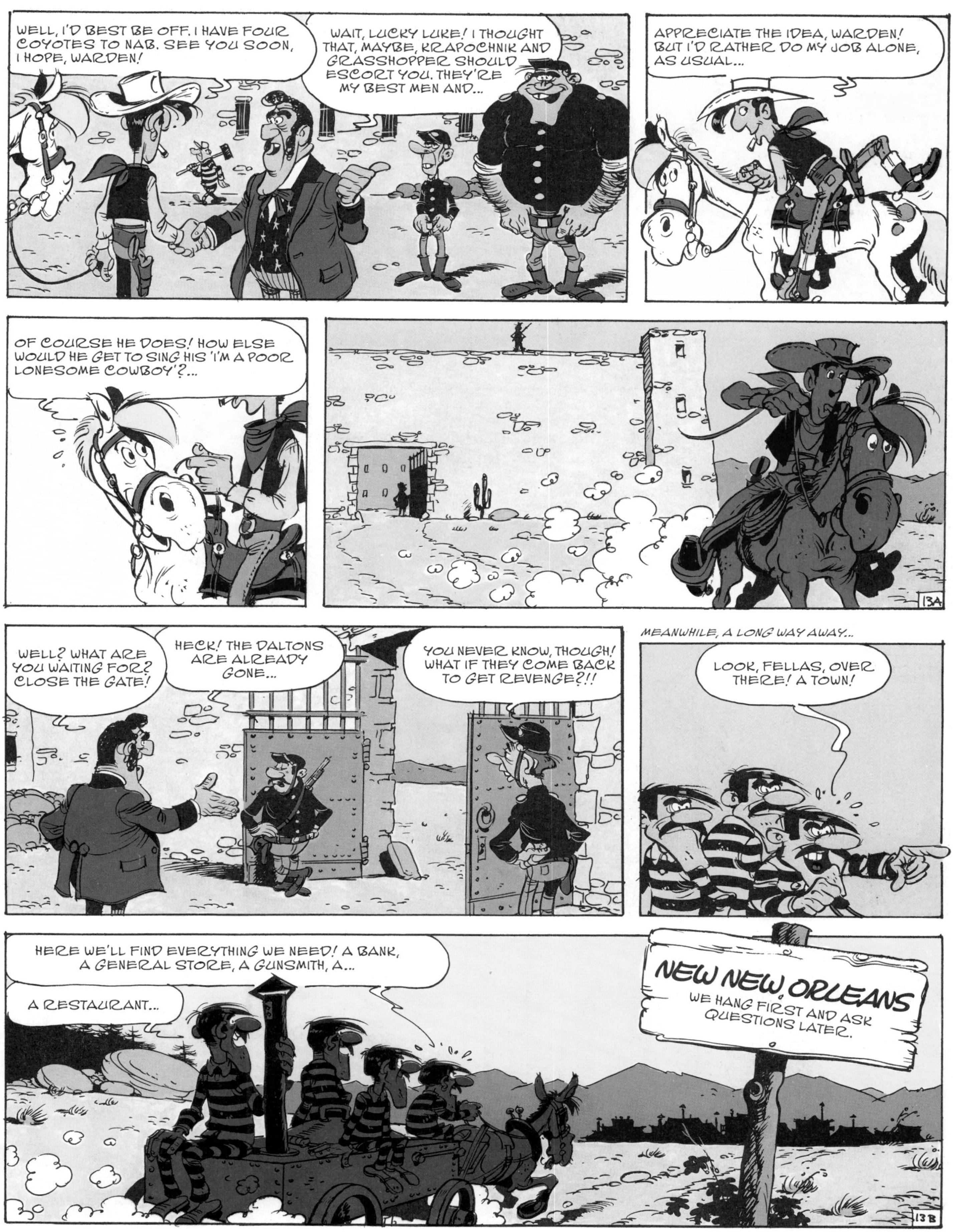
WELL, I'D BEST BE OFF. I HAVE FOUR COYOTES TO NAB. SEE YOU SOON, I HOPE, WARDEN!
WAIT, LUCKY LUKE! I THOUGHT THAT, MAYBE, KRAPOCHNIK AND GRASSHOPPER SHOULD ESCORT YOU. THEY'RE MY BEST MEN AND...
APPRECIATE THE IDEA, WARDEN! BUT I'D RATHER DO MY JOB ALONE, AS USUAL...
OF COURSE HE DOES! HOW ELSE WOULD HE GET TO SING HIS 'I'M A POOR LONESOME COWBOY'?...
13A
WELL? WHAT ARE YOU WAITING FOR? CLOSE THE GATE!
HECK! THE DALTONS ARE ALREADY GONE...
YOU NEVER KNOW, THOUGH! WHAT IF THEY COME BACK TO GET REVENGE?!!
MEANWHILE, A LONG WAY AWAY...
LOOK, FELLAS, OVER THERE! A TOWN!
HERE WE'LL FIND EVERYTHING WE NEED! A BANK, A GENERAL STORE, A GUNSMITH, A...
A RESTAURANT...
NEW NEW ORLEANS
WE HANG FIRST AND ASK QUESTIONS LATER.
13B

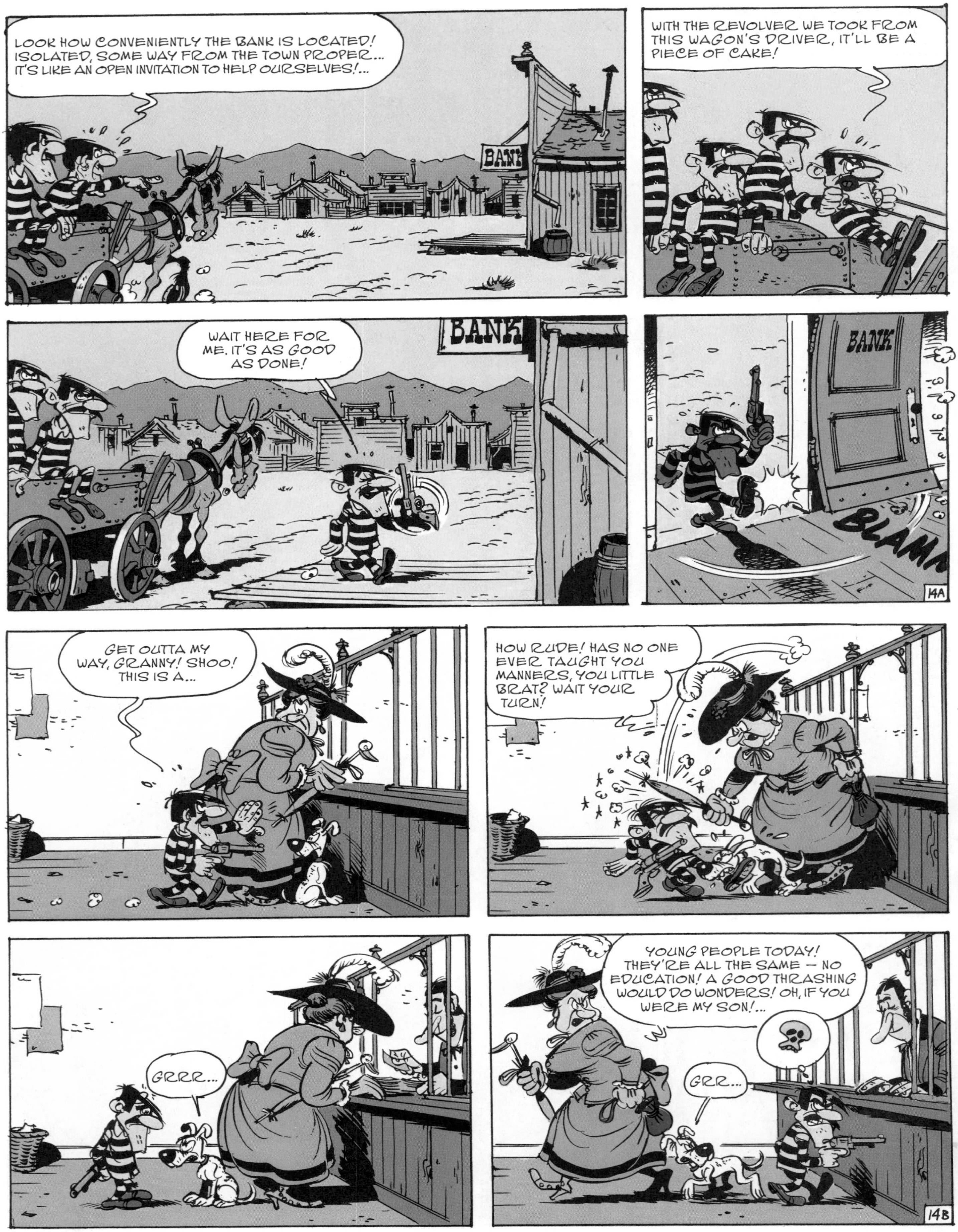

LOOK HOW CONVENIENTLY THE BANK IS LOCATED! ISOLATED, SOME WAY FROM THE TOWN PROPER... IT'S LIKE AN OPEN INVITATION TO HELP OURSELVES!...
BANK
WITH THE REVOLVER WE TOOK FROM THIS WAGON'S DRIVER, IT'LL BE A PIECE OF CAKE!
WAIT HERE FOR ME. IT'S AS GOOD AS DONE!
BANK
BANK
BLAMM
14A
GET OUTTA MY WAY, GRANNY! SHOO! THIS IS A...
HOW RUDE! HAS NO ONE EVER TAUGHT YOU MANNERS, YOU LITTLE BRAT? WAIT YOUR TURN!
GRRR...
YOUNG PEOPLE TODAY! THEY'RE ALL THE SAME — NO EDUCATION! A GOOD THRASHING WOULD DO WONDERS! OH, IF YOU WERE MY SON!...
GRR...
14B

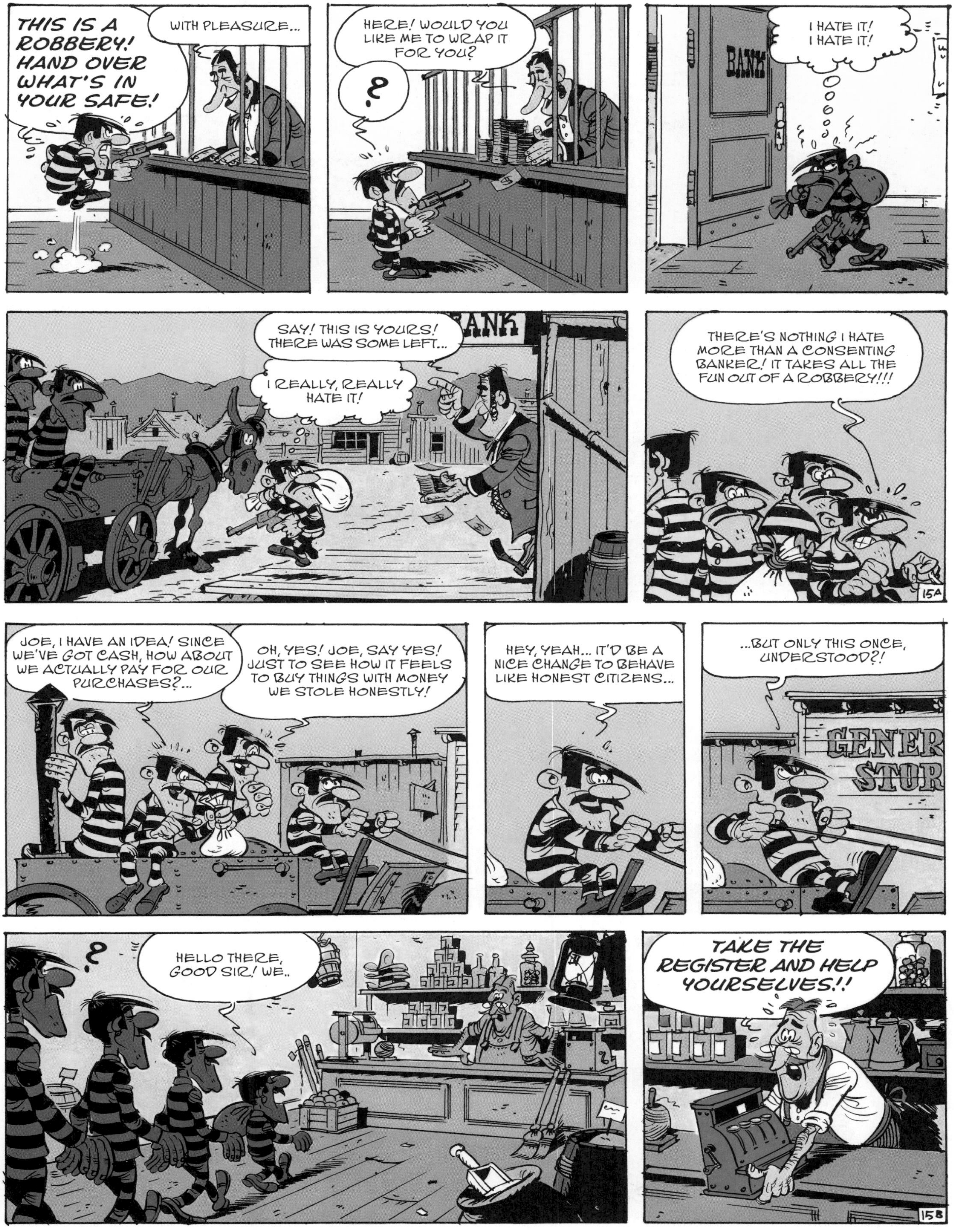
THIS IS A ROBBERY! HAND OVER WHAT'S IN YOUR SAFE!
WITH PLEASURE...
HERE! WOULD YOU LIKE ME TO WRAP IT FOR YOU?
?
I HATE IT! I HATE IT!
BANK
SAY! THIS IS YOURS! THERE WAS SOME LEFT...
I REALLY, REALLY HATE IT!
THERE'S NOTHING I HATE MORE THAN A CONSENTING BANKER! IT TAKES ALL THE FUN OUT OF A ROBBERY!!!
15A
JOE, I HAVE AN IDEA! SINCE WE'VE GOT CASH, HOW ABOUT WE ACTUALLY PAY FOR OUR PURCHASES?...
OH, YES! JOE, SAY YES! JUST TO SEE HOW IT FEELS TO BUY THINGS WITH MONEY WE STOLE HONESTLY!
HEY, YEAH... IT'D BE A NICE CHANGE TO BEHAVE LIKE HONEST CITIZENS...
...BUT ONLY THIS ONCE, UNDERSTOOD?!
?
HELLO THERE, GOOD SIR! WE..
TAKE THE REGISTER AND HELP YOURSELVES!!
15B

WHAT'S GOT INTO YOU? WE HAVE MONEY AND EVERY INTENTION TO PAY! WE STOPPED AT THE BANK AND...

I'M SORRY, IT'S JUST... YOUR CLOTHES...

WHAT ABOUT OUR CLOTHES? IS THERE A LAW THAT FORBIDS PEOPLE FROM WEARING STRIPED CLOTHING NOW?

NO, NO, OF COURSE NOT!

SO, THAT'S EIGHT REVOLVERS WITH BELTS AND AMMUNITION, A SELECTION OF CLOTHES AND A CAN OF BEANS... THAT'S 51 DOLLARS EXACTLY!

SEVENTEEN NOTES — THERE YOU GO!

16A

WAIT!

AH, HE WANTS TO GIVE US A LITTLE SOMETHING FOR FREE. I'LL TAKE ANOTHER CAN OF BEANS!

YOUR BANKNOTES ARE FAKE!

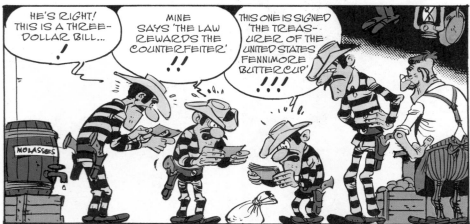

HE'S RIGHT! THIS IS A THREE-DOLLAR BILL...!

MINE SAYS 'THE LAW REWARDS THE COUNTERFEITER'!!

THIS ONE IS SIGNED 'THE TREAS-URER OF THE UNITED STATES FENNIMORE BUTTERCUP'!!!

THAT NO-GOOD, ROTTEN SKUNK OF A FORGER.!!

16B

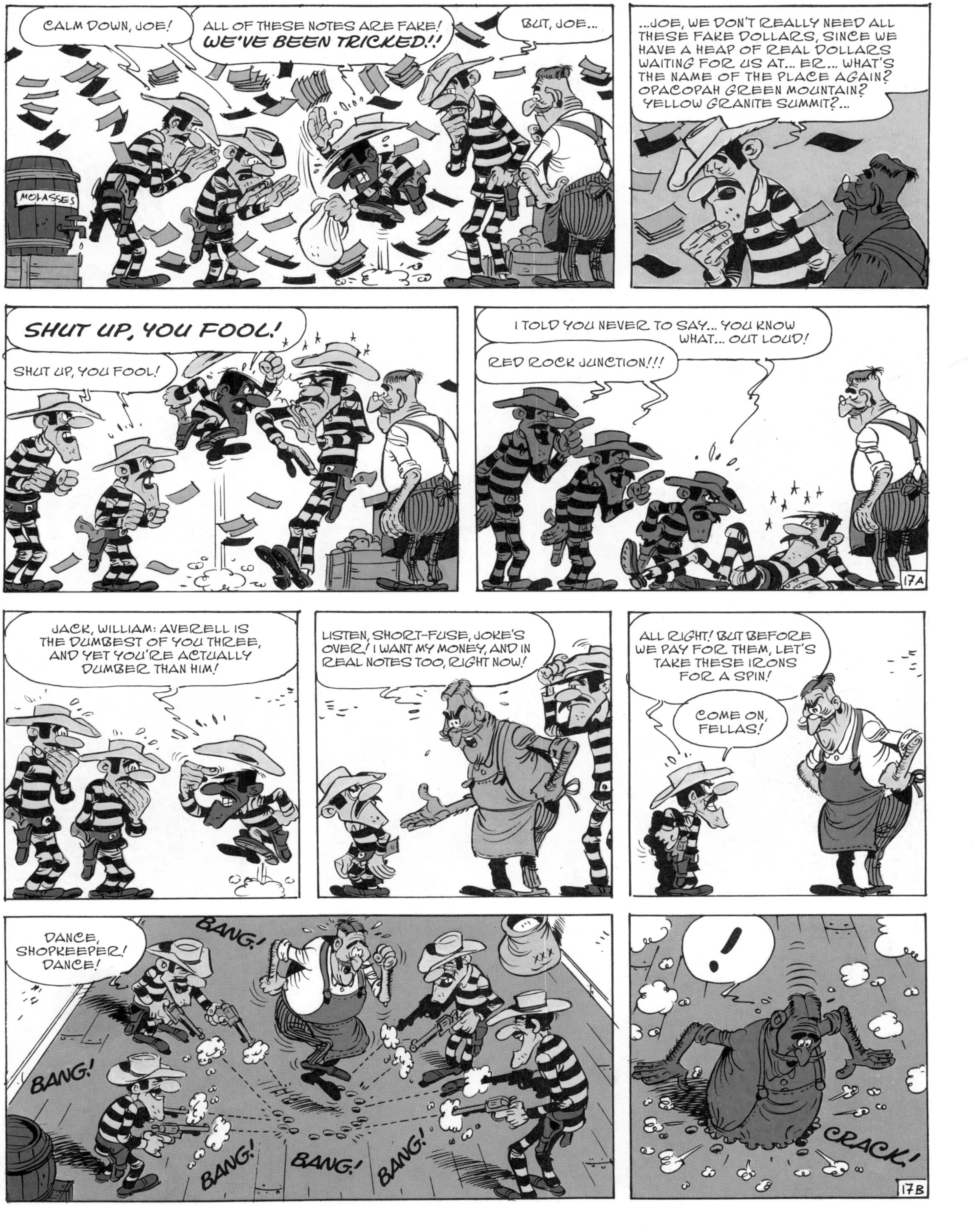
CALM DOWN, JOE!
ALL OF THESE NOTES ARE FAKE! WE'VE BEEN TRICKED!!
BUT, JOE...
MOLASSES
...JOE, WE DON'T REALLY NEED ALL THESE FAKE DOLLARS, SINCE WE HAVE A HEAP OF REAL DOLLARS WAITING FOR US AT... ER... WHAT'S THE NAME OF THE PLACE AGAIN? OPACOPAH GREEN MOUNTAIN? YELLOW GRANITE SUMMIT?...
SHUT UP, YOU FOOL!
SHUT UP, YOU FOOL!
I TOLD YOU NEVER TO SAY... YOU KNOW WHAT... OUT LOUD!
RED ROCK JUNCTION!!!
17A
JACK, WILLIAM: AVERELL IS THE DUMBEST OF YOU THREE, AND YET YOU'RE ACTUALLY DUMBER THAN HIM!
LISTEN, SHORT-FUSE, JOKE'S OVER! I WANT MY MONEY, AND IN REAL NOTES TOO, RIGHT NOW!
ALL RIGHT! BUT BEFORE WE PAY FOR THEM, LET'S TAKE THESE IRONS FOR A SPIN!
COME ON, FELLAS!
DANCE, SHOPKEEPER! DANCE!
BANG!
BANG!
BANG!
BANG!
BANG!
!
CRACK!
17B

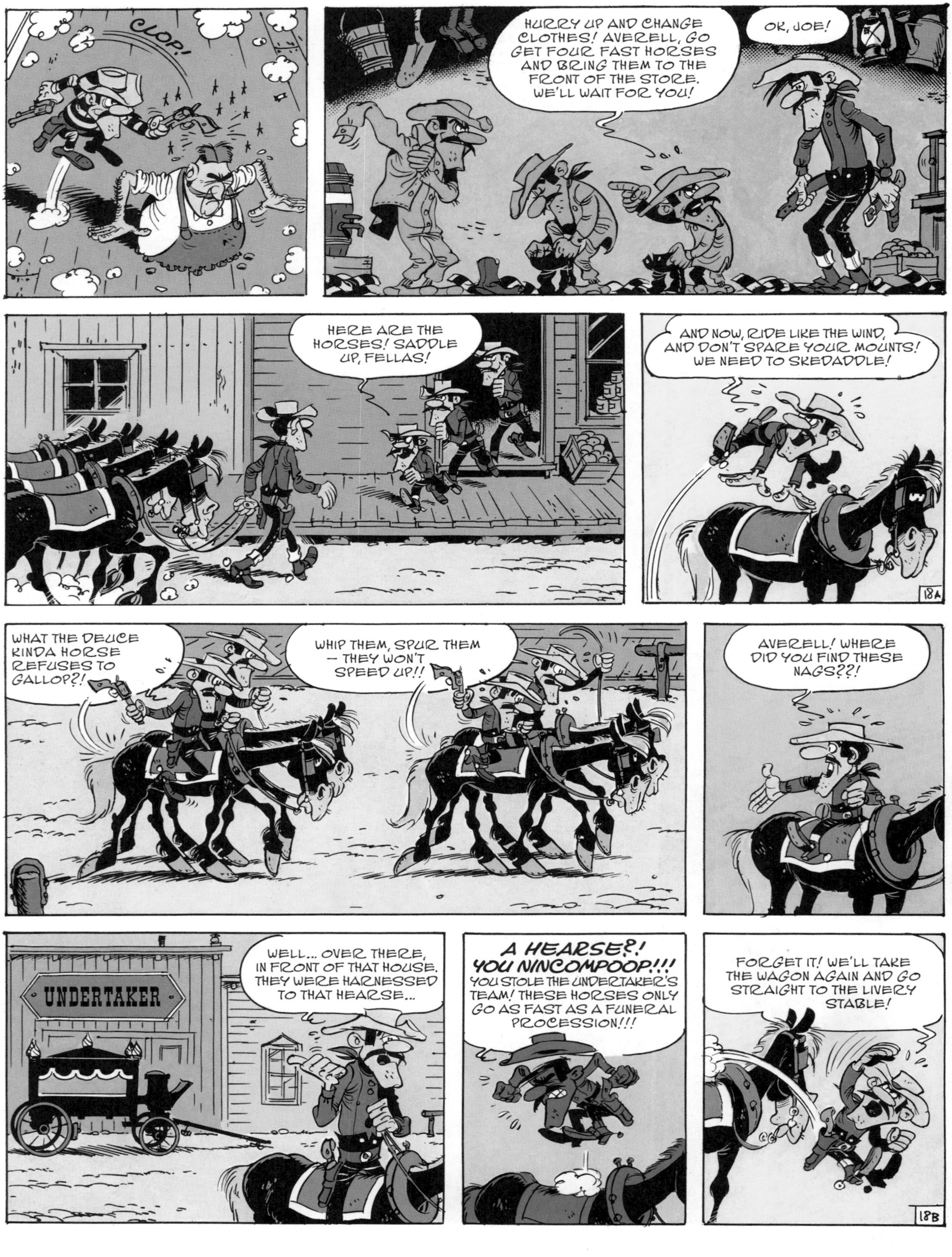
CLOP!
HURRY UP AND CHANGE CLOTHES! AVERELL, GO GET FOUR FAST HORSES AND BRING THEM TO THE FRONT OF THE STORE. WE'LL WAIT FOR YOU!
OK, JOE!
HERE ARE THE HORSES! SADDLE UP, FELLAS!
AND NOW, RIDE LIKE THE WIND, AND DON'T SPARE YOUR MOUNTS! WE NEED TO SKEDADDLE!
WHAT THE DEUCE KINDA HORSE REFUSES TO GALLOP?!
WHIP THEM, SPUR THEM — THEY WON'T SPEED UP!!
AVERELL! WHERE DID YOU FIND THESE NAGS??!
UNDERTAKER
WELL... OVER THERE, IN FRONT OF THAT HOUSE. THEY WERE HARNESSED TO THAT HEARSE...
A HEARSE?! YOU NINCOMPOOP!!! YOU STOLE THE UNDERTAKER'S TEAM! THESE HORSES ONLY GO AS FAST AS A FUNERAL PROCESSION!!!
FORGET IT! WE'LL TAKE THE WAGON AGAIN AND GO STRAIGHT TO THE LIVERY STABLE!

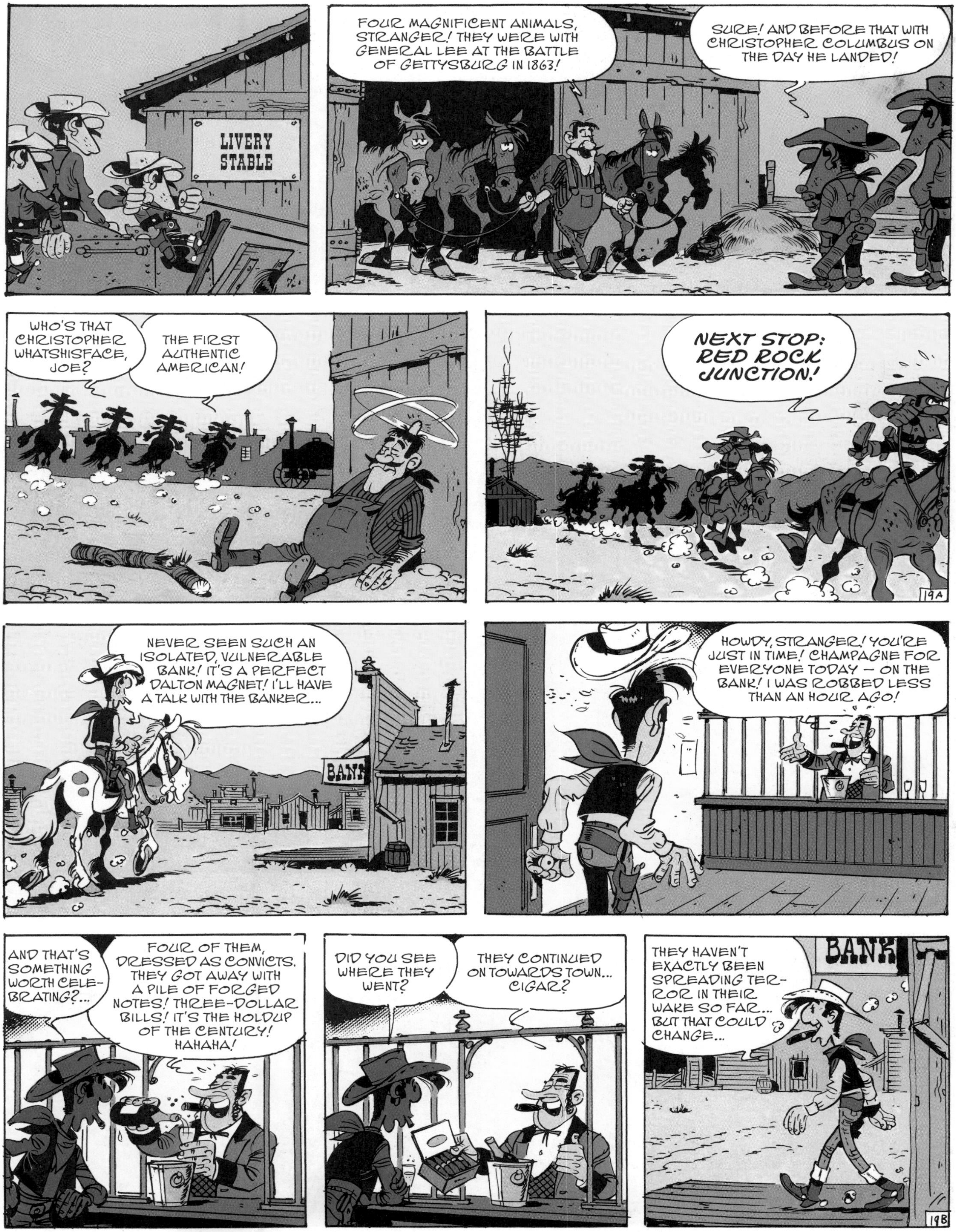
LIVERY STABLE
FOUR MAGNIFICENT ANIMALS, STRANGER! THEY WERE WITH GENERAL LEE AT THE BATTLE OF GETTYSBURG IN 1863!
SURE! AND BEFORE THAT WITH CHRISTOPHER COLUMBUS ON THE DAY HE LANDED!
WHO'S THAT CHRISTOPHER WHATSHISFACE, JOE?
THE FIRST AUTHENTIC AMERICAN!
NEXT STOP: RED ROCK JUNCTION!
19A
NEVER SEEN SUCH AN ISOLATED, VULNERABLE BANK! IT'S A PERFECT DALTON MAGNET! I'LL HAVE A TALK WITH THE BANKER...
HOWDY, STRANGER! YOU'RE JUST IN TIME! CHAMPAGNE FOR EVERYONE TODAY – ON THE BANK! I WAS ROBBED LESS THAN AN HOUR AGO!
AND THAT'S SOMETHING WORTH CELEBRATING?...
FOUR OF THEM, DRESSED AS CONVICTS. THEY GOT AWAY WITH A PILE OF FORGED NOTES! THREE-DOLLAR BILLS! IT'S THE HOLDUP OF THE CENTURY! HAHAHA!
DID YOU SEE WHERE THEY WENT?
THEY CONTINUED ON TOWARDS TOWN... CIGAR?
BANK
THEY HAVEN'T EXACTLY BEEN SPREADING TERROR IN THEIR WAKE SO FAR... BUT THAT COULD CHANGE...
19B

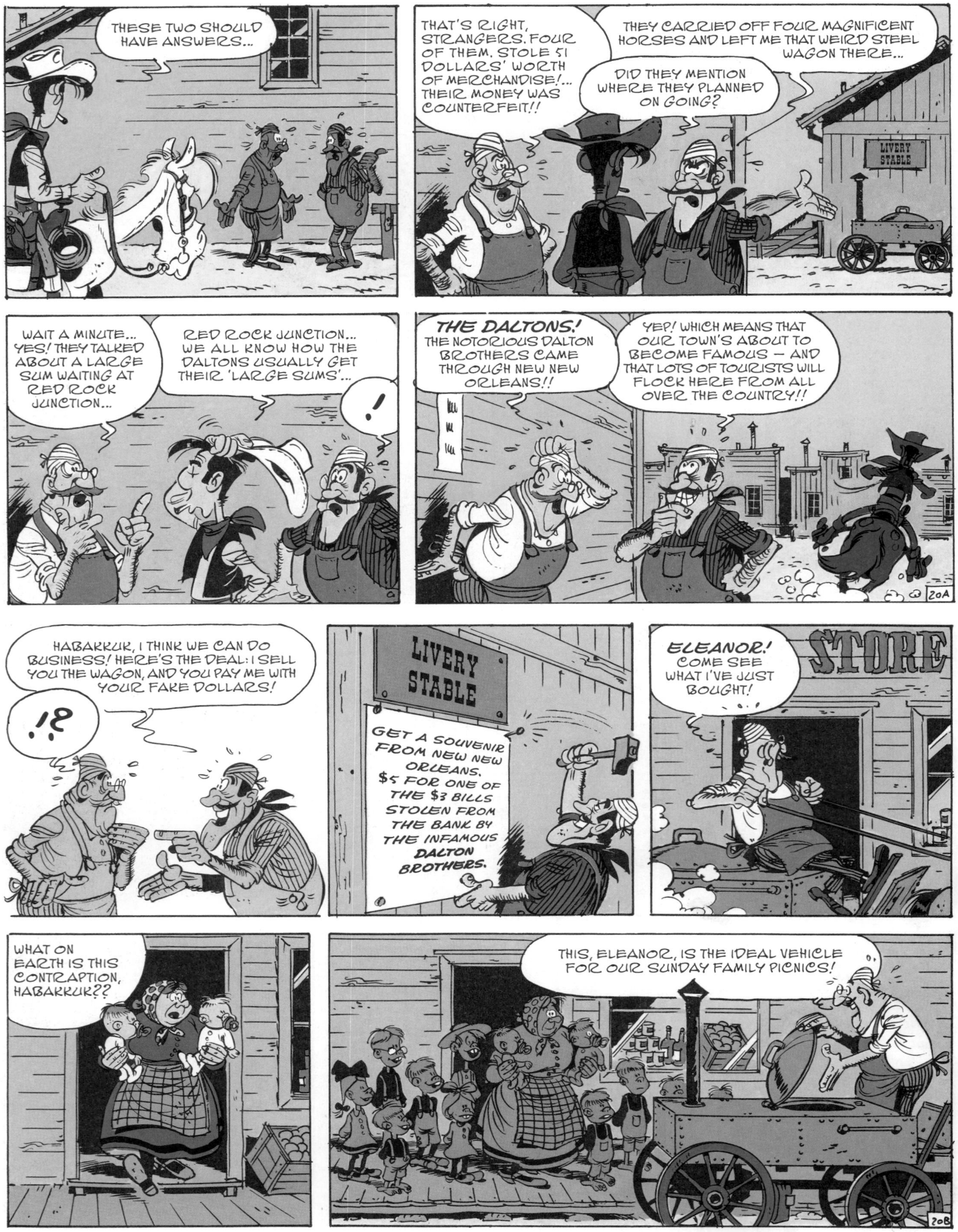
THESE TWO SHOULD HAVE ANSWERS...
THAT'S RIGHT, STRANGERS. FOUR OF THEM. STOLE 51 DOLLARS' WORTH OF MERCHANDISE!... THEIR MONEY WAS COUNTERFEIT!!
THEY CARRIED OFF FOUR MAGNIFICENT HORSES AND LEFT ME THAT WEIRD STEEL WAGON THERE...
DID THEY MENTION WHERE THEY PLANNED ON GOING?
LIVERY STABLE
WAIT A MINUTE... YES! THEY TALKED ABOUT A LARGE SUM WAITING AT RED ROCK JUNCTION...
RED ROCK JUNCTION... WE ALL KNOW HOW THE DALTONS USUALLY GET THEIR 'LARGE SUMS'...
!
THE DALTONS! THE NOTORIOUS DALTON BROTHERS CAME THROUGH NEW NEW ORLEANS!!
YEP! WHICH MEANS THAT OUR TOWN'S ABOUT TO BECOME FAMOUS — AND THAT LOTS OF TOURISTS WILL FLOCK HERE FROM ALL OVER THE COUNTRY!!
20A
HABAKKUK, I THINK WE CAN DO BUSINESS! HERE'S THE DEAL: I SELL YOU THE WAGON, AND YOU PAY ME WITH YOUR FAKE DOLLARS!
!?
LIVERY STABLE
GET A SOUVENIR FROM NEW NEW ORLEANS. $5 FOR ONE OF THE $3 BILLS STOLEN FROM THE BANK BY THE INFAMOUS DALTON BROTHERS.
STORE
ELEANOR! COME SEE WHAT I'VE JUST BOUGHT!
WHAT ON EARTH IS THIS CONTRAPTION, HABAKKUK??
THIS, ELEANOR, IS THE IDEAL VEHICLE FOR OUR SUNDAY FAMILY PICNICS!
20B

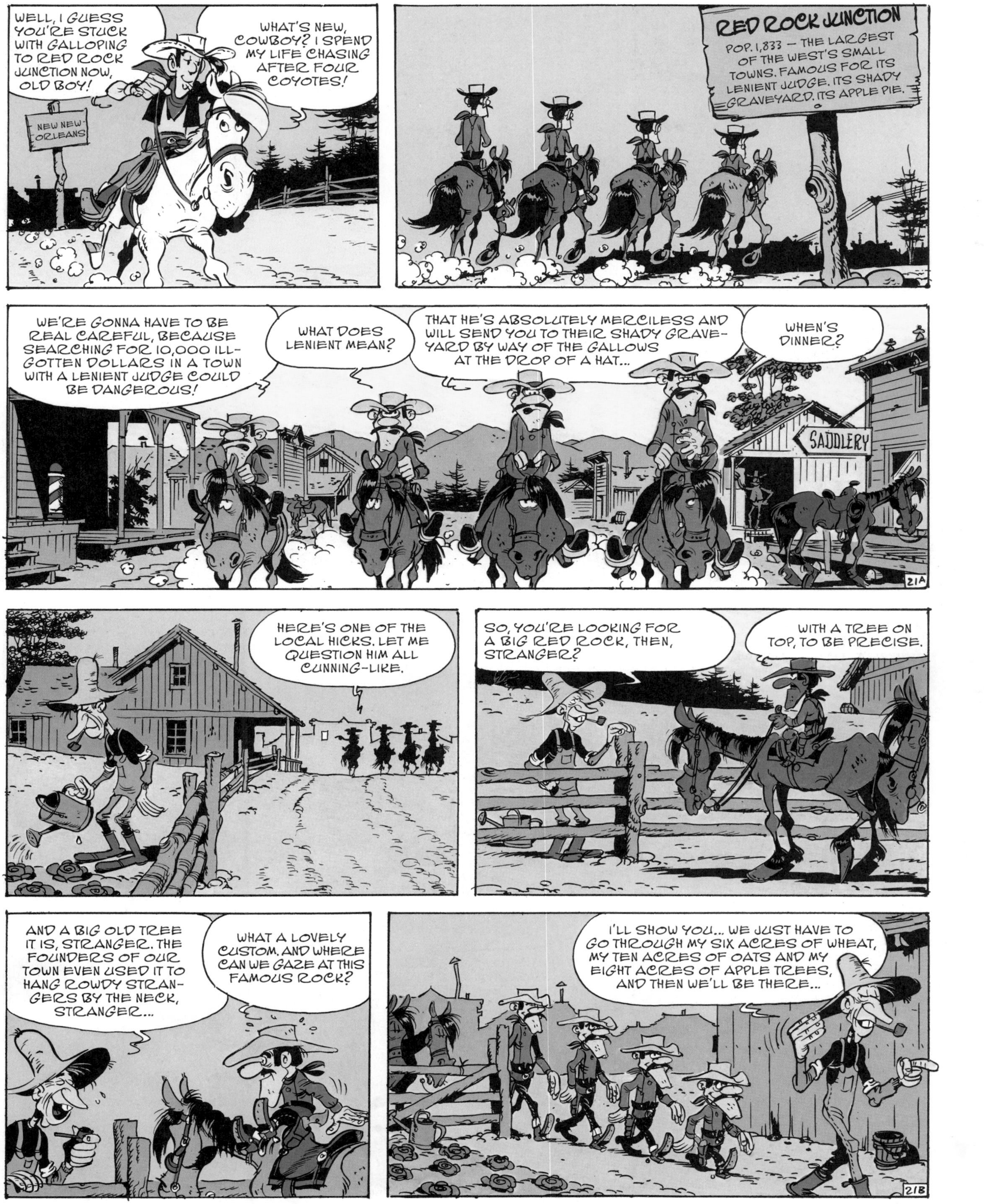
WELL, I GUESS YOU'RE STUCK WITH GALLOPING TO RED ROCK JUNCTION NOW, OLD BOY!
WHAT'S NEW, COWBOY? I SPEND MY LIFE CHASING AFTER FOUR COYOTES!
NEW NEW-ORLEANS
RED ROCK JUNCTION
POP. 1,833 — THE LARGEST OF THE WEST'S SMALL TOWNS. FAMOUS FOR ITS LENIENT JUDGE, ITS SHADY GRAVEYARD, ITS APPLE PIE.
WE'RE GONNA HAVE TO BE REAL CAREFUL, BECAUSE SEARCHING FOR 10,000 ILL-GOTTEN DOLLARS IN A TOWN WITH A LENIENT JUDGE COULD BE DANGEROUS!
WHAT DOES LENIENT MEAN?
THAT HE'S ABSOLUTELY MERCILESS AND WILL SEND YOU TO THEIR SHADY GRAVE-YARD BY WAY OF THE GALLOWS AT THE DROP OF A HAT...
WHEN'S DINNER?
SADDLERY
21A
HERE'S ONE OF THE LOCAL HICKS. LET ME QUESTION HIM ALL CUNNING-LIKE.
SO, YOU'RE LOOKING FOR A BIG RED ROCK, THEN, STRANGER?
WITH A TREE ON TOP, TO BE PRECISE.
AND A BIG OLD TREE IT IS, STRANGER. THE FOUNDERS OF OUR TOWN EVEN USED IT TO HANG ROWDY STRANGERS BY THE NECK, STRANGER...
WHAT A LOVELY CUSTOM. AND WHERE CAN WE GAZE AT THIS FAMOUS ROCK?
I'LL SHOW YOU... WE JUST HAVE TO GO THROUGH MY SIX ACRES OF WHEAT, MY TEN ACRES OF OATS AND MY EIGHT ACRES OF APPLE TREES, AND THEN WE'LL BE THERE...
21B

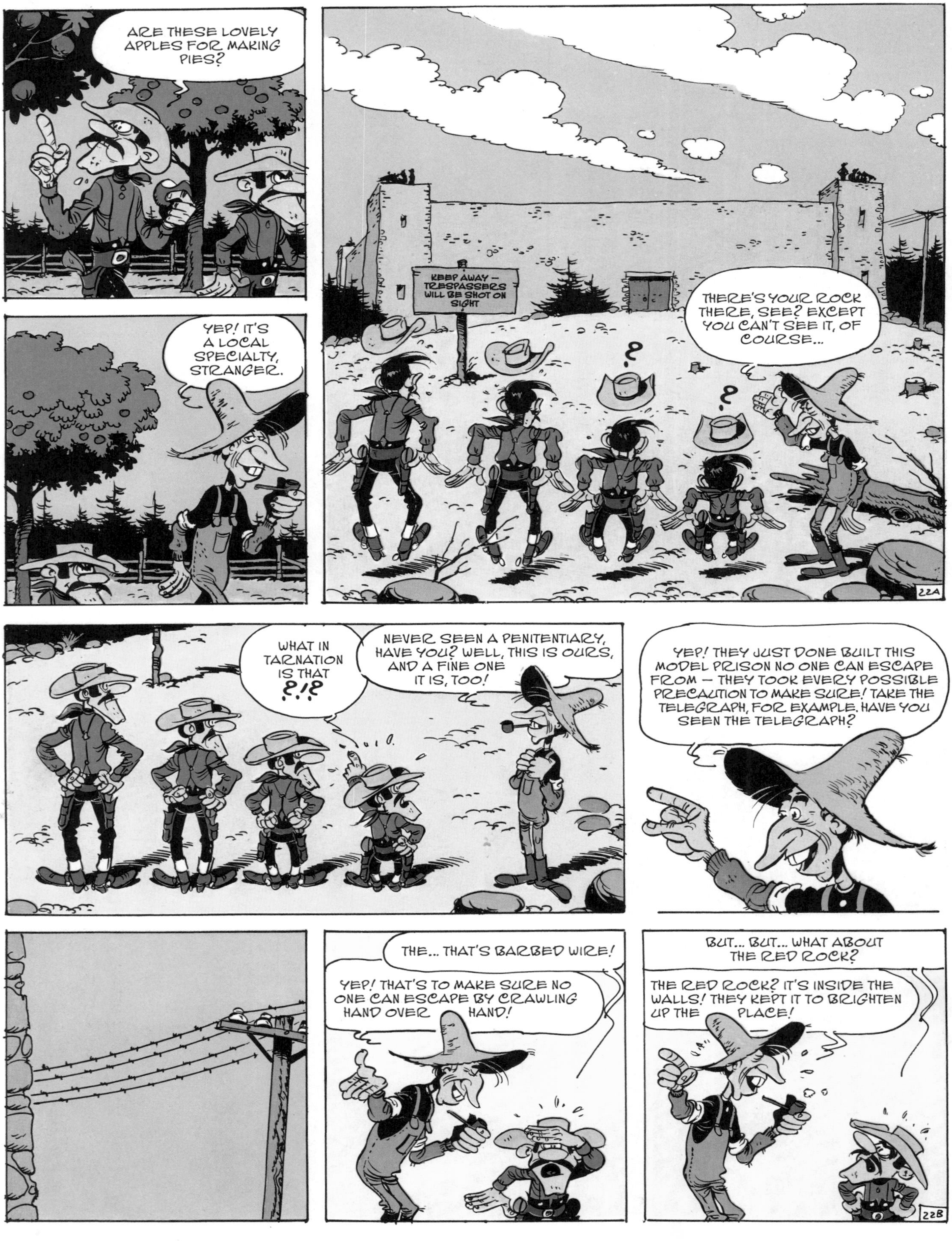
ARE THESE LOVELY APPLES FOR MAKING PIES?
YEP! IT'S A LOCAL SPECIALTY, STRANGER.
KEEP AWAY — TRESPASSERS WILL BE SHOT ON SIGHT
THERE'S YOUR ROCK THERE, SEE? EXCEPT YOU CAN'T SEE IT, OF COURSE...
?
?
22A
WHAT IN TARNATION IS THAT ?!?
NEVER SEEN A PENITENTIARY, HAVE YOU? WELL, THIS IS OURS, AND A FINE ONE IT IS, TOO!
YEP! THEY JUST DONE BUILT THIS MODEL PRISON NO ONE CAN ESCAPE FROM — THEY TOOK EVERY POSSIBLE PRECAUTION TO MAKE SURE! TAKE THE TELEGRAPH, FOR EXAMPLE. HAVE YOU SEEN THE TELEGRAPH?
THE... THAT'S BARBED WIRE!
YEP! THAT'S TO MAKE SURE NO ONE CAN ESCAPE BY CRAWLING HAND OVER HAND!
BUT... BUT... WHAT ABOUT THE RED ROCK?
THE RED ROCK? IT'S INSIDE THE WALLS! THEY KEPT IT TO BRIGHTEN UP THE PLACE!
22B

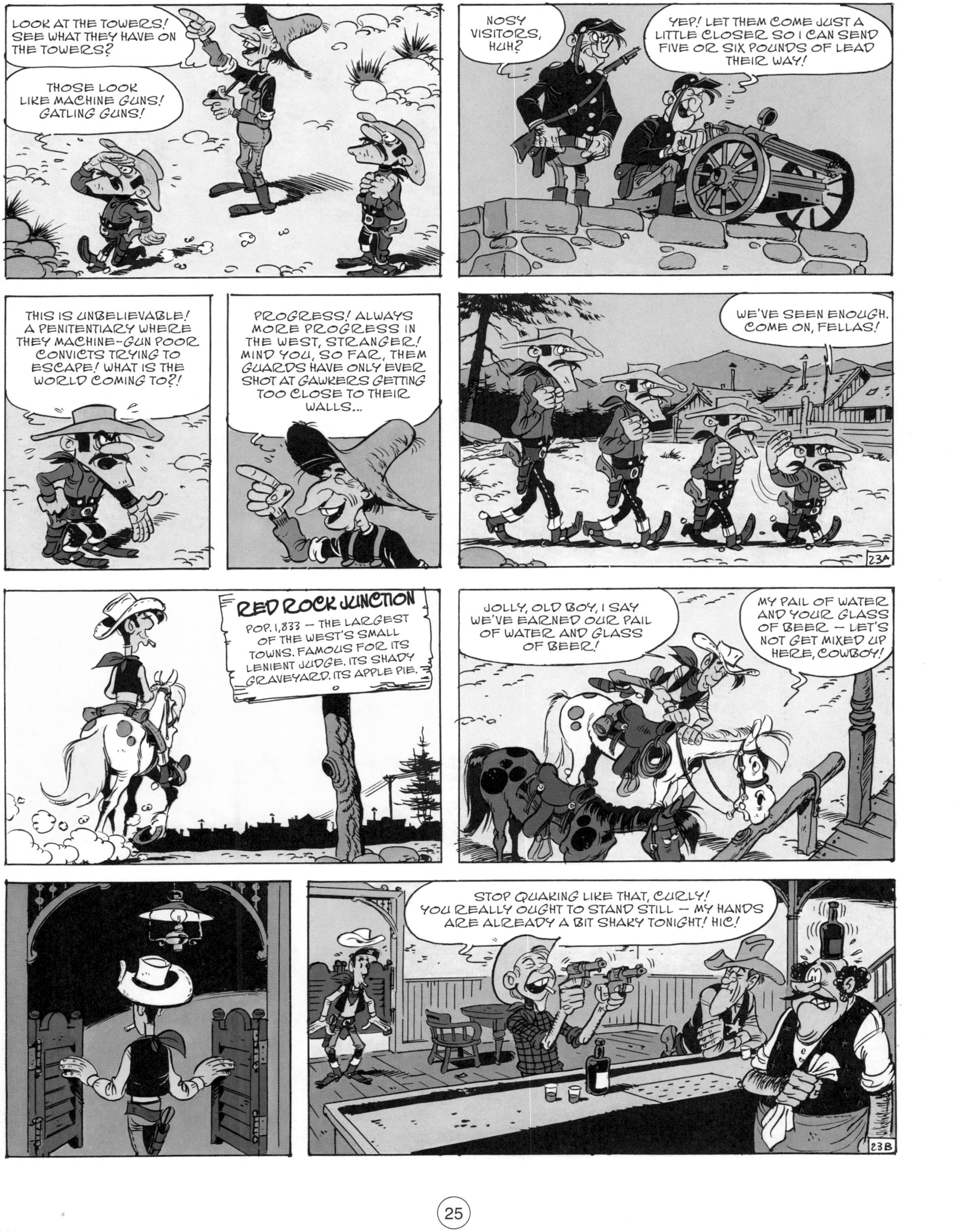

LOOK AT THE TOWERS! SEE WHAT THEY HAVE ON THE TOWERS?
THOSE LOOK LIKE MACHINE GUNS! GATLING GUNS!
NOSY VISITORS, HUH?
YEP! LET THEM COME JUST A LITTLE CLOSER SO I CAN SEND FIVE OR SIX POUNDS OF LEAD THEIR WAY!
THIS IS UNBELIEVABLE! A PENITENTIARY WHERE THEY MACHINE-GUN POOR CONVICTS TRYING TO ESCAPE! WHAT IS THE WORLD COMING TO?!
PROGRESS! ALWAYS MORE PROGRESS IN THE WEST, STRANGER! MIND YOU, SO FAR, THEM GUARDS HAVE ONLY EVER SHOT AT GAWKERS GETTING TOO CLOSE TO THEIR WALLS...
WE'VE SEEN ENOUGH. COME ON, FELLAS!
23A
RED ROCK JUNCTION
POP. 1,833 – THE LARGEST OF THE WEST'S SMALL TOWNS. FAMOUS FOR ITS LENIENT JUDGE. ITS SHADY GRAVEYARD. ITS APPLE PIE.
JOLLY, OLD BOY, I SAY WE'VE EARNED OUR PAIL OF WATER AND GLASS OF BEER!
MY PAIL OF WATER AND YOUR GLASS OF BEER – LET'S NOT GET MIXED UP HERE, COWBOY!
STOP QUAKING LIKE THAT, CURLY! YOU REALLY OUGHT TO STAND STILL – MY HANDS ARE ALREADY A BIT SHAKY TONIGHT! HIC!
23B

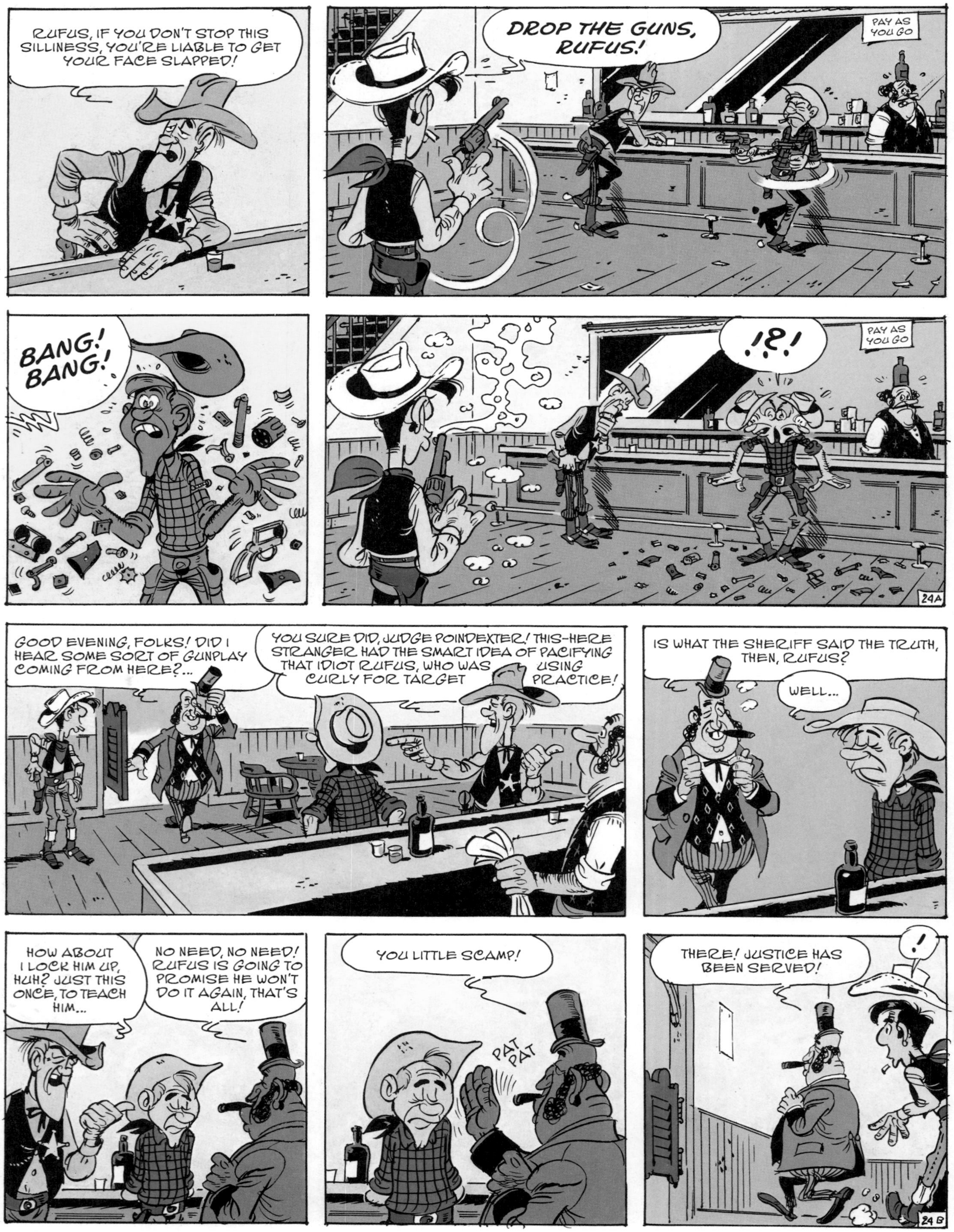
RUFUS, IF YOU DON'T STOP THIS SILLINESS, YOU'RE LIABLE TO GET YOUR FACE SLAPPED!
DROP THE GUNS, RUFUS!
PAY AS YOU GO
BANG! BANG!
!?!
PAY AS YOU GO
24A
GOOD EVENING, FOLKS! DID I HEAR SOME SORT OF GUNPLAY COMING FROM HERE?...
YOU SURE DID, JUDGE POINDEXTER! THIS-HERE STRANGER HAD THE SMART IDEA OF PACIFYING THAT IDIOT RUFUS, WHO WAS USING CURLY FOR TARGET PRACTICE!
IS WHAT THE SHERIFF SAID THE TRUTH, THEN, RUFUS?
WELL...
HOW ABOUT I LOCK HIM UP, HUH? JUST THIS ONCE, TO TEACH HIM...
NO NEED, NO NEED! RUFUS IS GOING TO PROMISE HE WON'T DO IT AGAIN, THAT'S ALL!
YOU LITTLE SCAMP!
PAT PAT
THERE! JUSTICE HAS BEEN SERVED!
!
24B

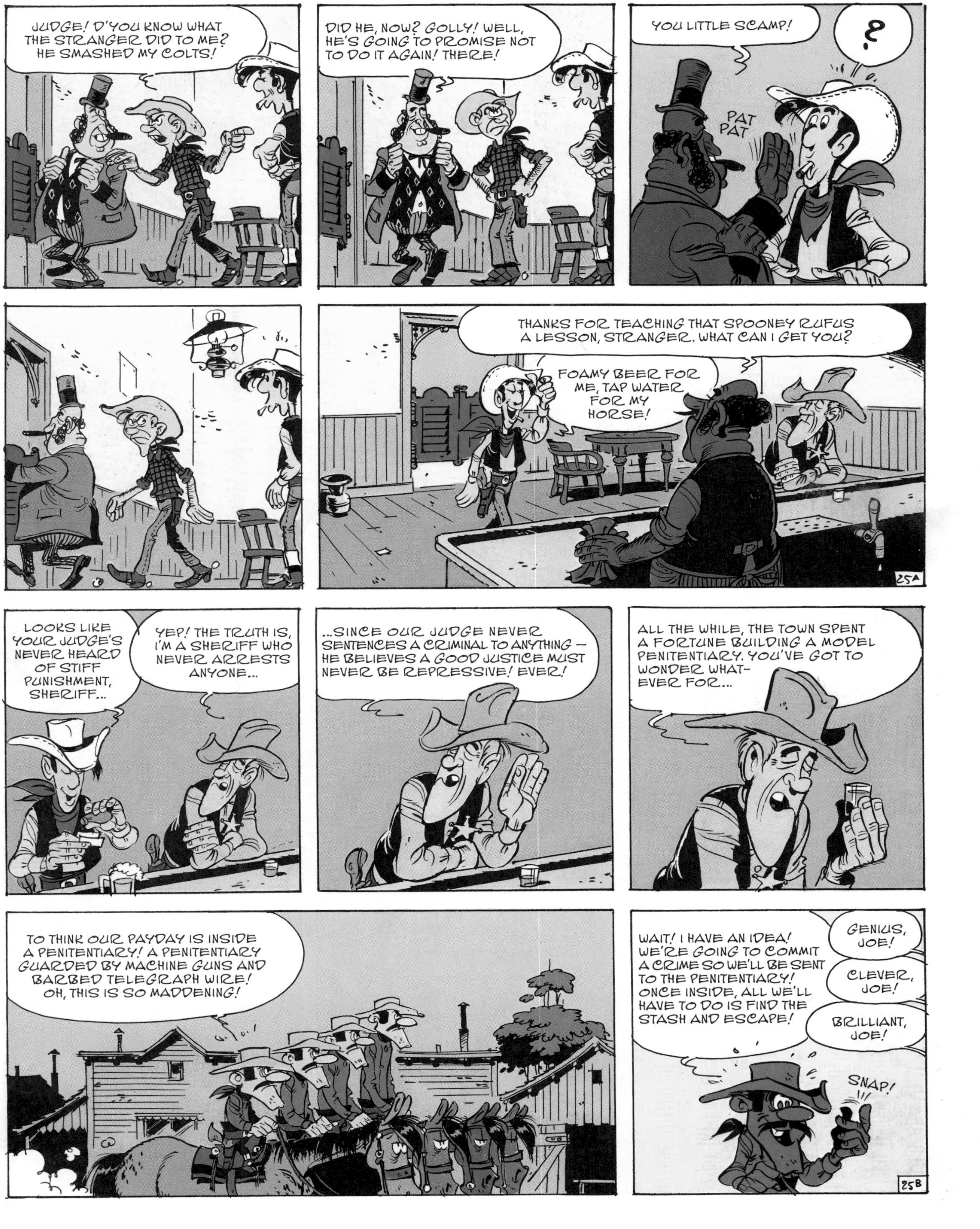

JUDGE! D'YOU KNOW WHAT THE STRANGER DID TO ME? HE SMASHED MY COLTS!
DID HE, NOW? GOLLY! WELL, HE'S GOING TO PROMISE NOT TO DO IT AGAIN! THERE!
YOU LITTLE SCAMP!
?
PAT PAT
THANKS FOR TEACHING THAT SPOONEY RUFUS A LESSON, STRANGER. WHAT CAN I GET YOU?
FOAMY BEER FOR ME, TAP WATER FOR MY HORSE!
25A
LOOKS LIKE YOUR JUDGE'S NEVER HEARD OF STIFF PUNISHMENT, SHERIFF...
YEP! THE TRUTH IS, I'M A SHERIFF WHO NEVER ARRESTS ANYONE...
...SINCE OUR JUDGE NEVER SENTENCES A CRIMINAL TO ANYTHING — HE BELIEVES A GOOD JUSTICE MUST NEVER BE REPRESSIVE! EVER!
ALL THE WHILE, THE TOWN SPENT A FORTUNE BUILDING A MODEL PENITENTIARY. YOU'VE GOT TO WONDER WHAT-EVER FOR...
TO THINK OUR PAYDAY IS INSIDE A PENITENTIARY! A PENITENTIARY GUARDED BY MACHINE GUNS AND BARBED TELEGRAPH WIRE! OH, THIS IS SO MADDENING!
WAIT! I HAVE AN IDEA! WE'RE GOING TO COMMIT A CRIME SO WE'LL BE SENT TO THE PENITENTIARY! ONCE INSIDE, ALL WE'LL HAVE TO DO IS FIND THE STASH AND ESCAPE!
GENIUS, JOE!
CLEVER, JOE!
BRILLIANT, JOE!
SNAP!
25B

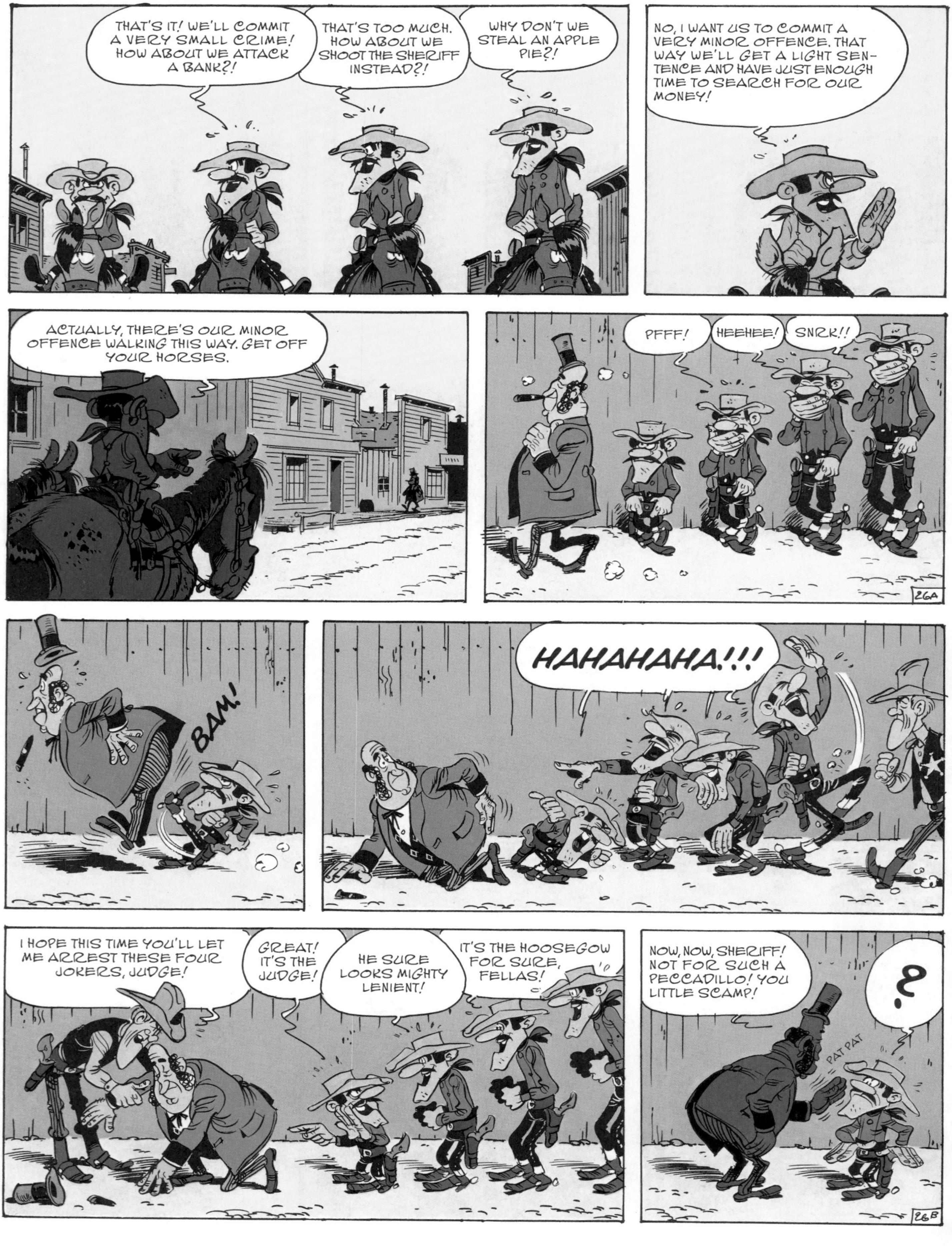
THAT'S IT! WE'LL COMMIT A VERY SMALL CRIME! HOW ABOUT WE ATTACK A BANK?!
THAT'S TOO MUCH. HOW ABOUT WE SHOOT THE SHERIFF INSTEAD?!
WHY DON'T WE STEAL AN APPLE PIE?!
NO, I WANT US TO COMMIT A VERY MINOR OFFENCE. THAT WAY WE'LL GET A LIGHT SENTENCE AND HAVE JUST ENOUGH TIME TO SEARCH FOR OUR MONEY!
ACTUALLY, THERE'S OUR MINOR OFFENCE WALKING THIS WAY. GET OFF YOUR HORSES.
PFFF!
HEEHEE!
SNRK!!
26A
BAM!
HAHAHAHA!!!
I HOPE THIS TIME YOU'LL LET ME ARREST THESE FOUR JOKERS, JUDGE!
GREAT! IT'S THE JUDGE!
HE SURE LOOKS MIGHTY LENIENT!
IT'S THE HOOSEGOW FOR SURE, FELLAS!
NOW, NOW, SHERIFF! NOT FOR SUCH A PECCADILLO! YOU LITTLE SCAMP!
?
PAT PAT
26B

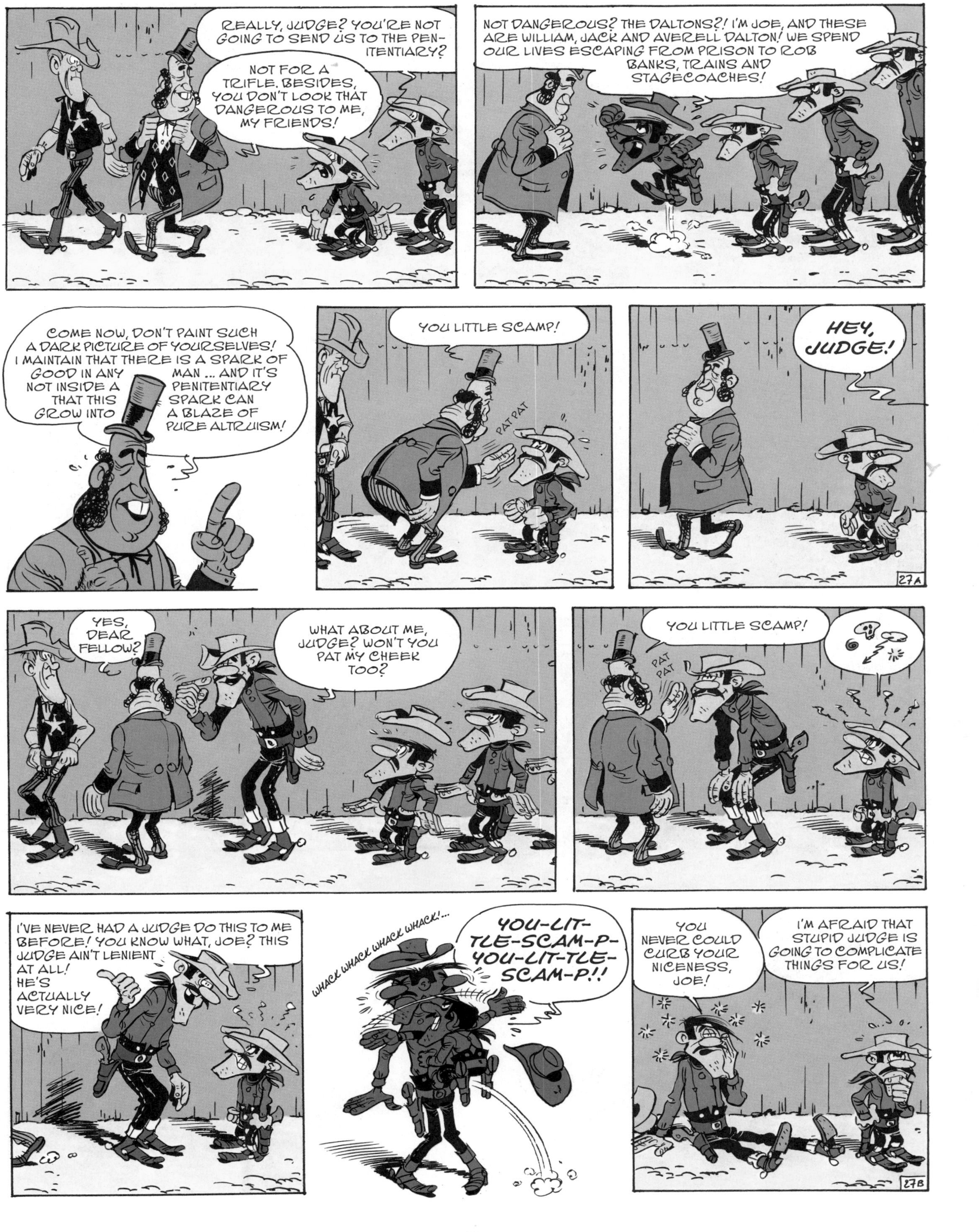
REALLY, JUDGE? YOU'RE NOT GOING TO SEND US TO THE PENITENTIARY?
NOT FOR A TRIFLE. BESIDES, YOU DON'T LOOK THAT DANGEROUS TO ME, MY FRIENDS!
NOT DANGEROUS? THE DALTONS?! I'M JOE, AND THESE ARE WILLIAM, JACK AND AVERELL DALTON! WE SPEND OUR LIVES ESCAPING FROM PRISON TO ROB BANKS, TRAINS AND STAGECOACHES!
COME NOW, DON'T PAINT SUCH A DARK PICTURE OF YOURSELVES! I MAINTAIN THAT THERE IS A SPARK OF GOOD IN ANY MAN ... AND IT'S NOT INSIDE A PENITENTIARY THAT THIS SPARK CAN GROW INTO A BLAZE OF PURE ALTRUISM!
YOU LITTLE SCAMP!
PAT PAT
HEY, JUDGE!
27A
YES, DEAR FELLOW?
WHAT ABOUT ME, JUDGE? WON'T YOU PAT MY CHEEK TOO?
YOU LITTLE SCAMP!
PAT PAT
I'VE NEVER HAD A JUDGE DO THIS TO ME BEFORE! YOU KNOW WHAT, JOE? THIS JUDGE AIN'T LENIENT AT ALL! HE'S ACTUALLY VERY NICE!
WHACK WHACK WHACK WHACK!...
YOU-LIT-TLE-SCAM-P-YOU-LIT-TLE-SCAM-P!!
YOU NEVER COULD CURB YOUR NICENESS, JOE!
I'M AFRAID THAT STUPID JUDGE IS GOING TO COMPLICATE THINGS FOR US!
27B

YOU LITTLE SCAMP! YOU LITTLE SCAMP! HEEHEEHEEHOHO!

STOP THIS TOMFOOLERY RIGHT NOW!!!

WE'RE GOING TO TAKE A ROOM AT THE HOTEL, WHERE I CAN THINK ABOUT HOW TO GET INSIDE THE PENITENTIARY! WE'VE BEEN LOCKED UP AGAINST OUR WILL DOZENS OF TIMES, BUT NOW THAT WE WANT TO GO TO JAIL, THEY WON'T LET US! JUSTICE MAKES NO SENSE!

THE DALTONS... NOW I REMEMBER SOME OLD WANTED POSTERS FOR THEM. YOU KNOW, THOSE FELLAS ARE SERIOUS CUSTOMERS, JUDGE!

THEN THEY'LL REFORM, SHERIFF! DID YOU SEE THE LOOK OF PURE CHILDISH JOY ON THE FACE OF THE TALLEST WHEN I SHOWED HIM SOME SYMPATHY?

TELEGRAM FOR YOU, JUDGE!

28A

?

BAD NEWS, JUDGE?

NOT EXACTLY... AN UNSIGNED MESSAGE ANNOUNCING THE ARRIVAL OF SOME SORT OF PACKAGE ON THE NEXT TRAIN. I AM CONFUSED, SHERIFF.

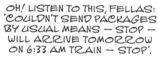

OH! LISTEN TO THIS, FELLAS: 'COULDN'T SEND PACKAGES BY USUAL MEANS — STOP — WILL ARRIVE TOMORROW ON 6:33 AM TRAIN — STOP'.

THERE'S AN IDEA! TOMORROW WE'LL ATTACK THE 6:33 TRAIN'S MAIL CAR!...

28B

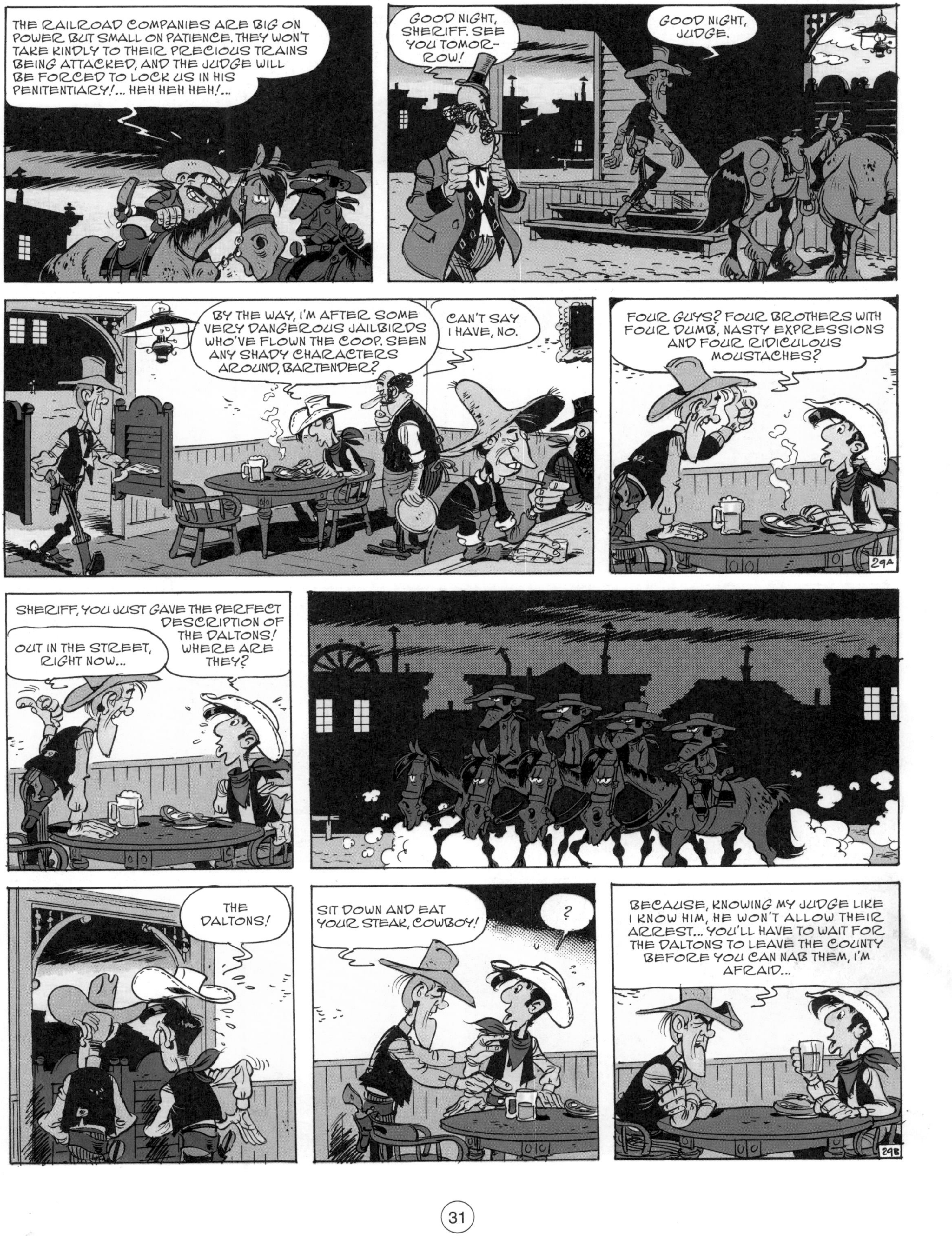
THE RAILROAD COMPANIES ARE BIG ON POWER BUT SMALL ON PATIENCE. THEY WON'T TAKE KINDLY TO THEIR PRECIOUS TRAINS BEING ATTACKED, AND THE JUDGE WILL BE FORCED TO LOCK US IN HIS PENITENTIARY!... HEH HEH HEH!...
GOOD NIGHT, SHERIFF. SEE YOU TOMOR-ROW!
GOOD NIGHT, JUDGE.
BY THE WAY, I'M AFTER SOME VERY DANGEROUS JAILBIRDS WHO'VE FLOWN THE COOP. SEEN ANY SHADY CHARACTERS AROUND, BARTENDER?
CAN'T SAY I HAVE, NO.
FOUR GUYS? FOUR BROTHERS WITH FOUR DUMB, NASTY EXPRESSIONS AND FOUR RIDICULOUS MOUSTACHES?
29A
SHERIFF, YOU JUST GAVE THE PERFECT DESCRIPTION OF THE DALTONS! WHERE ARE THEY?
OUT IN THE STREET, RIGHT NOW...
THE DALTONS!
SIT DOWN AND EAT YOUR STEAK, COWBOY!
?
BECAUSE, KNOWING MY JUDGE LIKE I KNOW HIM, HE WON'T ALLOW THEIR ARREST... YOU'LL HAVE TO WAIT FOR THE DALTONS TO LEAVE THE COUNTY BEFORE YOU CAN NAB THEM, I'M AFRAID...
29B

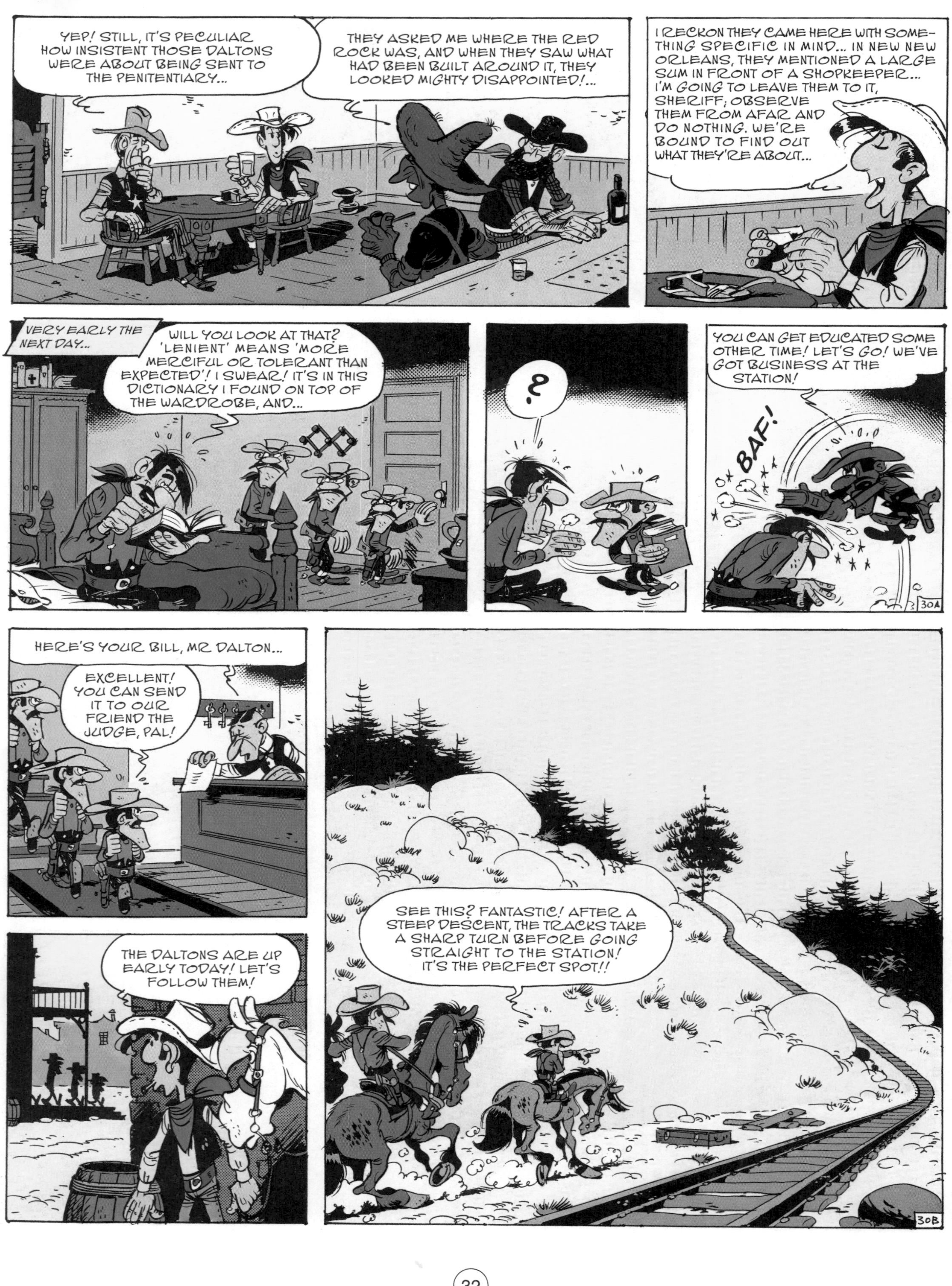
YEP! STILL, IT'S PECULIAR HOW INSISTENT THOSE DALTONS WERE ABOUT BEING SENT TO THE PENITENTIARY...
THEY ASKED ME WHERE THE RED ROCK WAS, AND WHEN THEY SAW WHAT HAD BEEN BUILT AROUND IT, THEY LOOKED MIGHTY DISAPPOINTED!...
I RECKON THEY CAME HERE WITH SOMETHING SPECIFIC IN MIND... IN NEW NEW ORLEANS, THEY MENTIONED A LARGE SUM IN FRONT OF A SHOPKEEPER... I'M GOING TO LEAVE THEM TO IT, SHERIFF; OBSERVE THEM FROM AFAR AND DO NOTHING. WE'RE BOUND TO FIND OUT WHAT THEY'RE ABOUT...
VERY EARLY THE NEXT DAY...
WILL YOU LOOK AT THAT? 'LENIENT' MEANS 'MORE MERCIFUL OR TOLERANT THAN EXPECTED'! I SWEAR! IT'S IN THIS DICTIONARY I FOUND ON TOP OF THE WARDROBE, AND...
?
YOU CAN GET EDUCATED SOME OTHER TIME! LET'S GO! WE'VE GOT BUSINESS AT THE STATION!
BAF!
30A
HERE'S YOUR BILL, MR DALTON...
EXCELLENT! YOU CAN SEND IT TO OUR FRIEND THE JUDGE, PAL!
THE DALTONS ARE UP EARLY TODAY! LET'S FOLLOW THEM!
SEE THIS? FANTASTIC! AFTER A STEEP DESCENT, THE TRACKS TAKE A SHARP TURN BEFORE GOING STRAIGHT TO THE STATION! IT'S THE PERFECT SPOT!!
30B

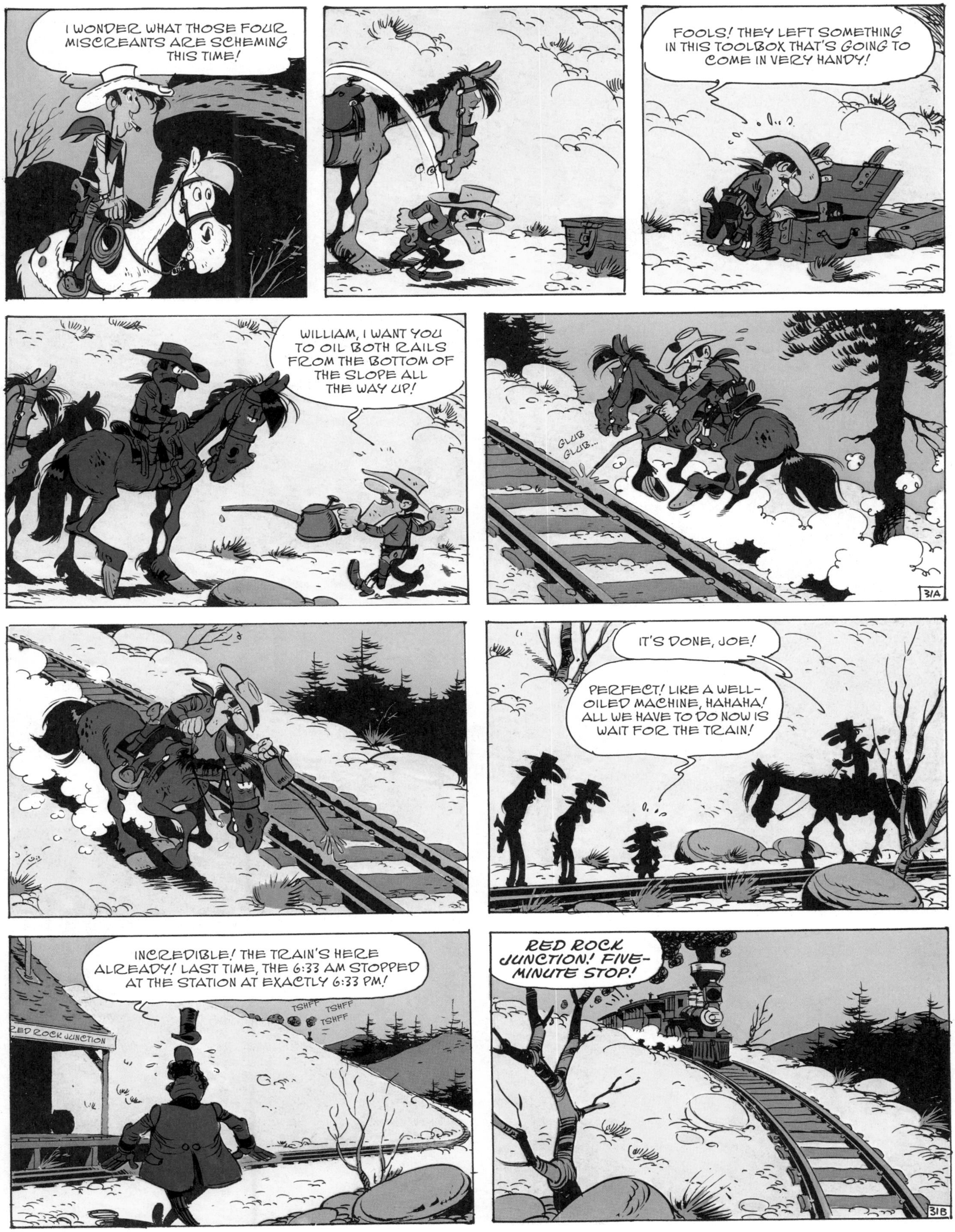
I WONDER WHAT THOSE FOUR MISCREANTS ARE SCHEMING THIS TIME!
FOOLS! THEY LEFT SOMETHING IN THIS TOOLBOX THAT'S GOING TO COME IN VERY HANDY!
WILLIAM, I WANT YOU TO OIL BOTH RAILS FROM THE BOTTOM OF THE SLOPE ALL THE WAY UP!
GLUB GLUB...
31A
IT'S DONE, JOE!
PERFECT! LIKE A WELL-OILED MACHINE, HAHAHA! ALL WE HAVE TO DO NOW IS WAIT FOR THE TRAIN!
INCREDIBLE! THE TRAIN'S HERE ALREADY! LAST TIME, THE 6:33 AM STOPPED AT THE STATION AT EXACTLY 6:33 PM!
TSHFF TSHFF TSHFF
RED ROCK JUNCTION
RED ROCK JUNCTION! FIVE-MINUTE STOP!
31B

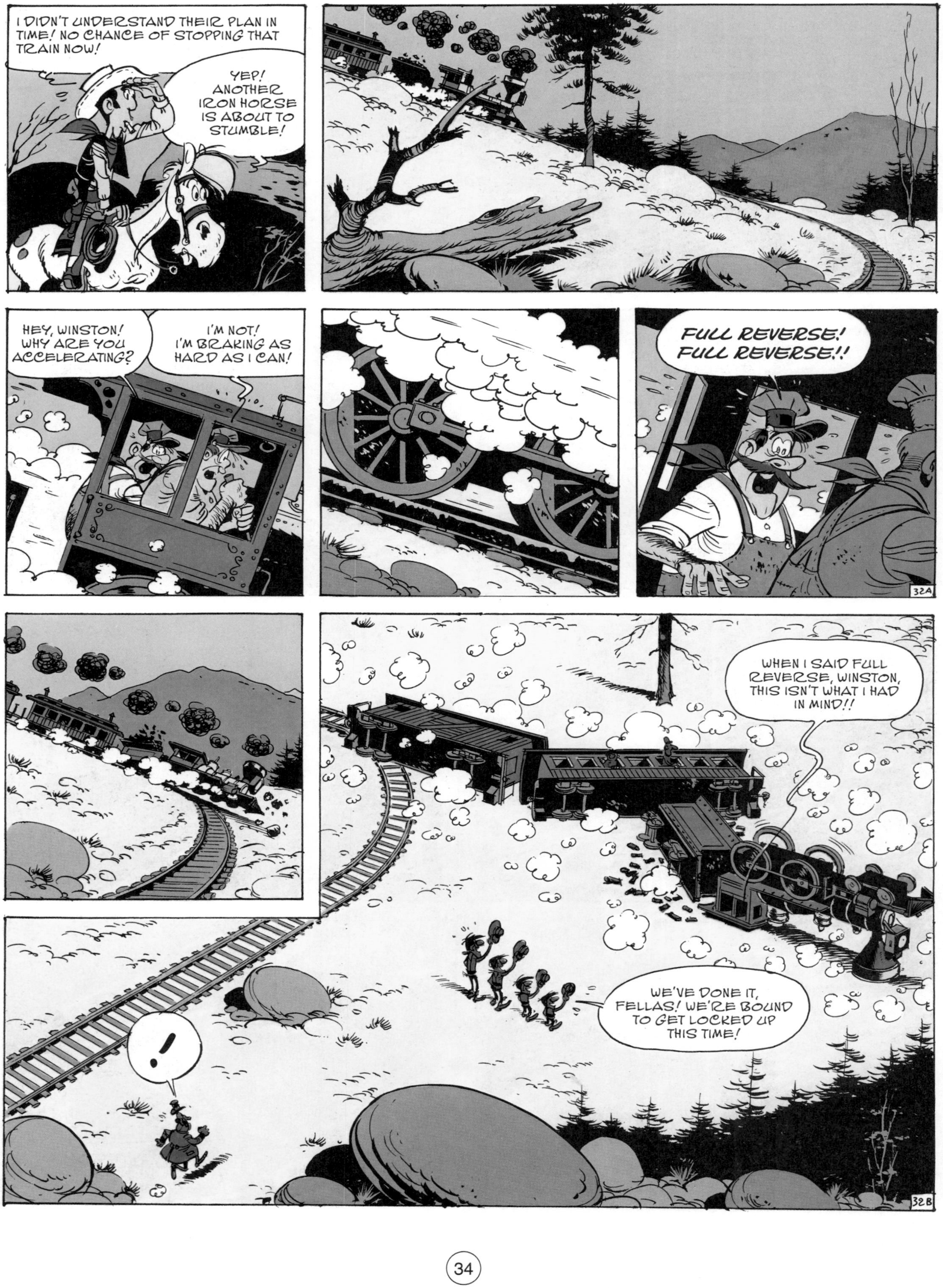

I DIDN'T UNDERSTAND THEIR PLAN IN TIME! NO CHANCE OF STOPPING THAT TRAIN NOW!
YEP! ANOTHER IRON HORSE IS ABOUT TO STUMBLE!
HEY, WINSTON! WHY ARE YOU ACCELERATING?
I'M NOT! I'M BRAKING AS HARD AS I CAN!
FULL REVERSE! FULL REVERSE!!
32A
WHEN I SAID FULL REVERSE, WINSTON, THIS ISN'T WHAT I HAD IN MIND!!
WE'VE DONE IT, FELLAS! WE'RE BOUND TO GET LOCKED UP THIS TIME!
!
32B

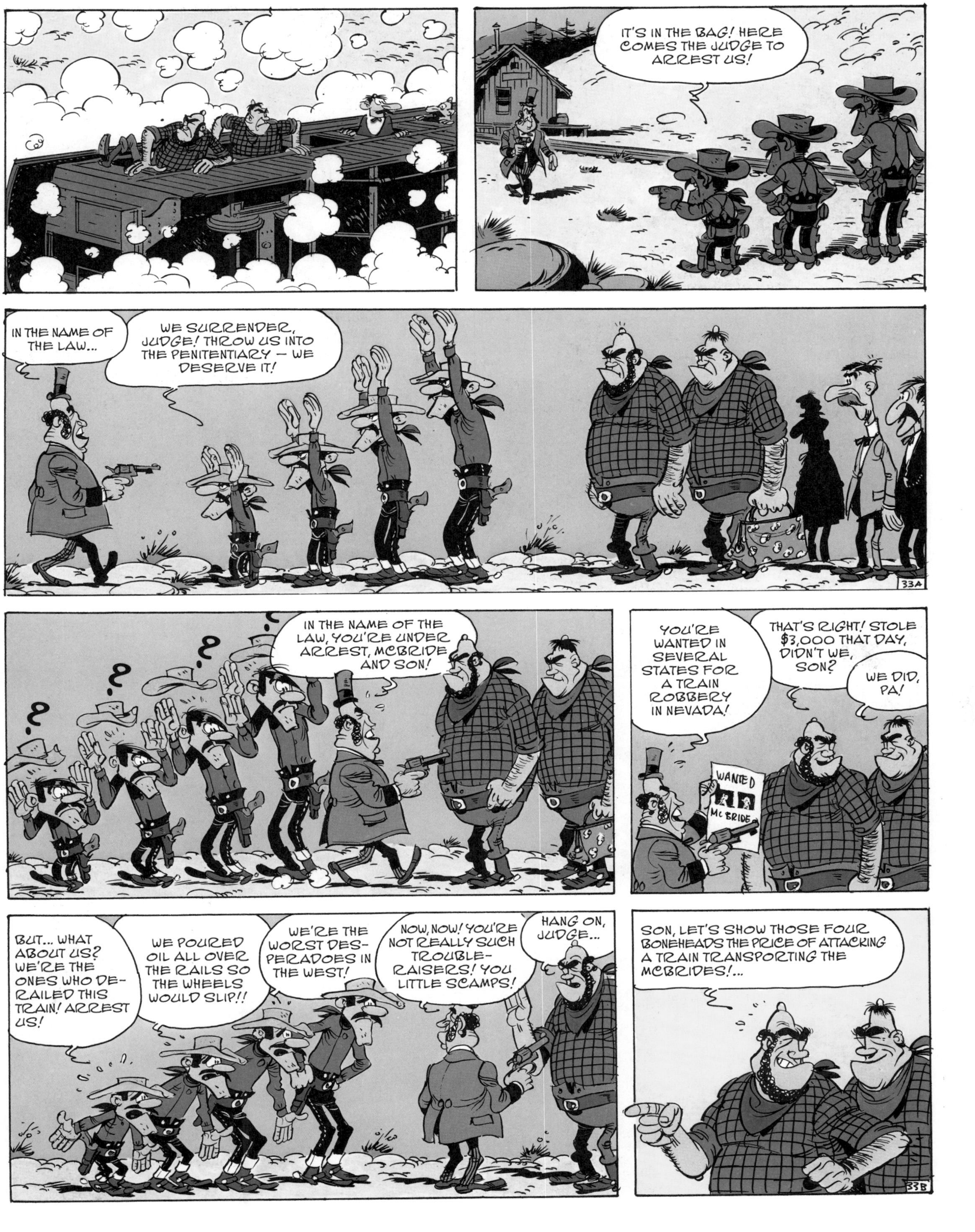

IT'S IN THE BAG! HERE COMES THE JUDGE TO ARREST US!
IN THE NAME OF THE LAW...
WE SURRENDER, JUDGE! THROW US INTO THE PENITENTIARY — WE DESERVE IT!
33A
IN THE NAME OF THE LAW, YOU'RE UNDER ARREST, MCBRIDE AND SON!
YOU'RE WANTED IN SEVERAL STATES FOR A TRAIN ROBBERY IN NEVADA!
THAT'S RIGHT! STOLE $3,000 THAT DAY, DIDN'T WE, SON?
WE DID, PA!
WANTED
Mc BRIDE
BUT... WHAT ABOUT US? WE'RE THE ONES WHO DERAILED THIS TRAIN! ARREST US!
WE POURED OIL ALL OVER THE RAILS SO THE WHEELS WOULD SLIP!!
WE'RE THE WORST DESPERADOES IN THE WEST!
NOW, NOW! YOU'RE NOT REALLY SUCH TROUBLE-RAISERS! YOU LITTLE SCAMPS!
HANG ON, JUDGE...
SON, LET'S SHOW THOSE FOUR BONEHEADS THE PRICE OF ATTACKING A TRAIN TRANSPORTING THE MCBRIDES!...
33B

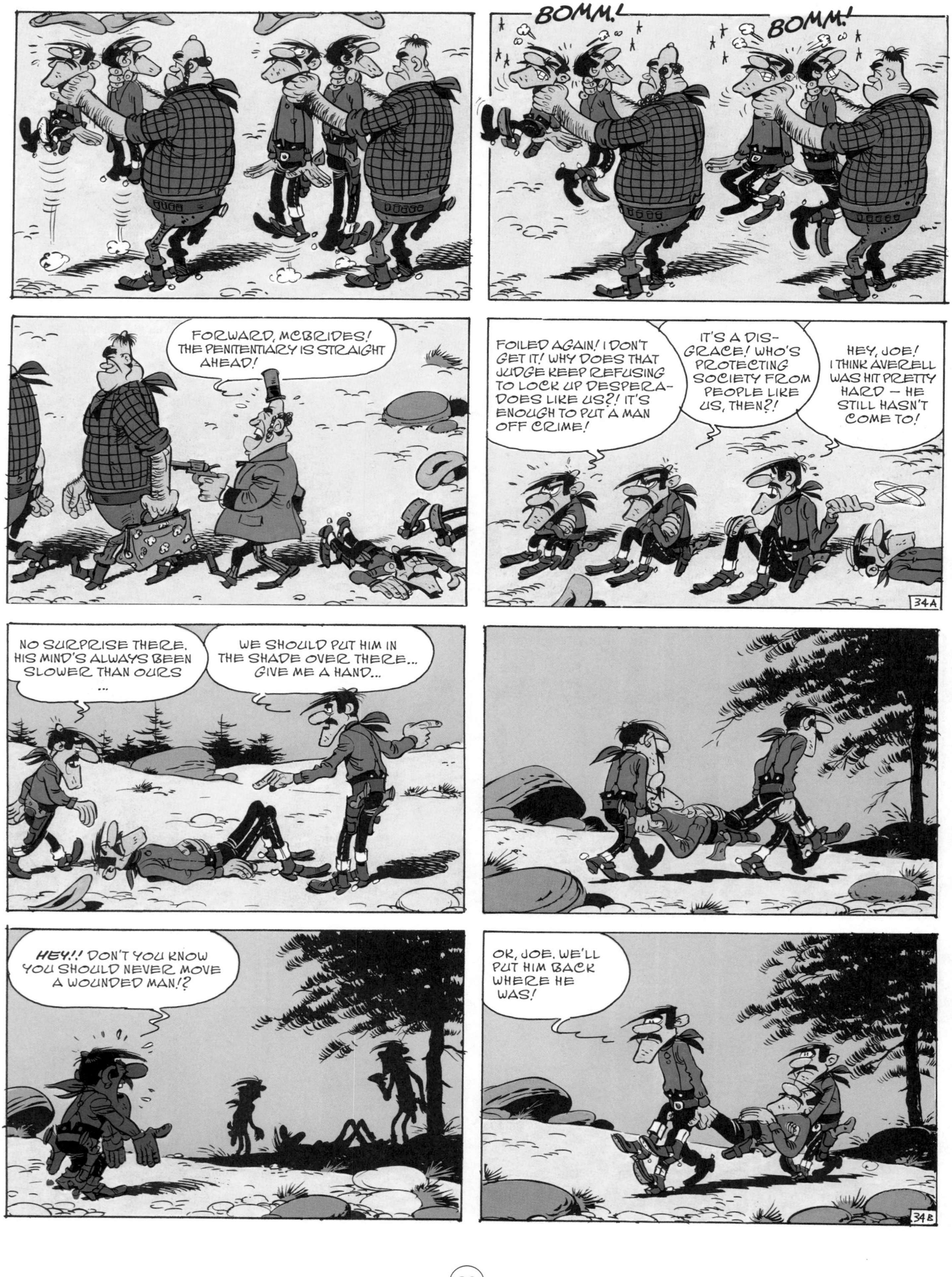
BOMM!
BOMM!
FORWARD, MCBRIDES! THE PENITENTIARY IS STRAIGHT AHEAD!
FOILED AGAIN! I DON'T GET IT! WHY DOES THAT JUDGE KEEP REFUSING TO LOCK UP DESPERADOES LIKE US?! IT'S ENOUGH TO PUT A MAN OFF CRIME!
IT'S A DISGRACE! WHO'S PROTECTING SOCIETY FROM PEOPLE LIKE US, THEN?!
HEY, JOE! I THINK AVERELL WAS HIT PRETTY HARD — HE STILL HASN'T COME TO!
34A
NO SURPRISE THERE. HIS MIND'S ALWAYS BEEN SLOWER THAN OURS ...
WE SHOULD PUT HIM IN THE SHADE OVER THERE... GIVE ME A HAND...
HEY!! DON'T YOU KNOW YOU SHOULD NEVER MOVE A WOUNDED MAN!?
OK, JOE. WE'LL PUT HIM BACK WHERE HE WAS!
34B

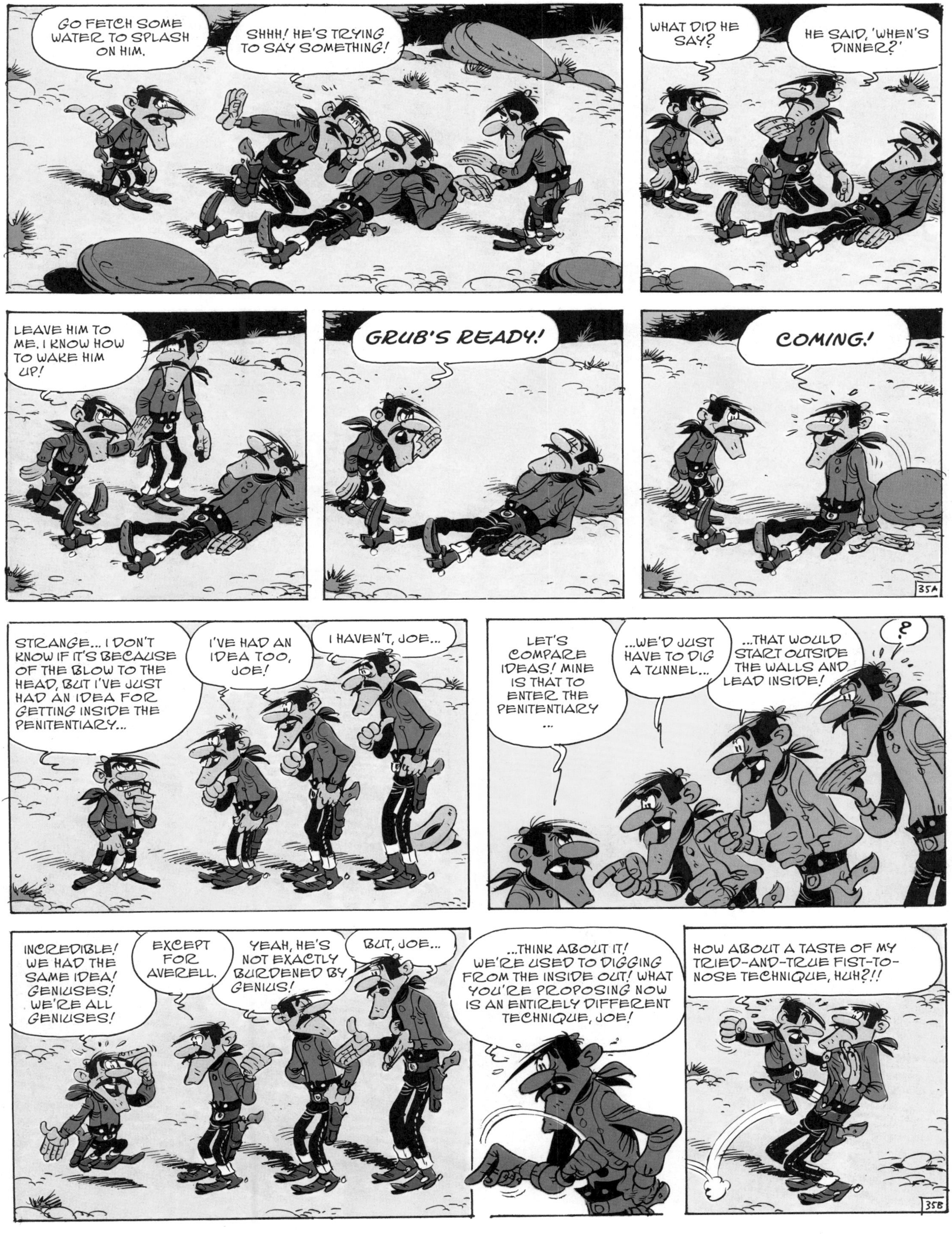
GO FETCH SOME WATER TO SPLASH ON HIM.
SHHH! HE'S TRYING TO SAY SOMETHING!
WHAT DID HE SAY?
HE SAID, 'WHEN'S DINNER?'
LEAVE HIM TO ME. I KNOW HOW TO WAKE HIM UP!
GRUB'S READY!
COMING!
35A
STRANGE... I DON'T KNOW IF IT'S BECAUSE OF THE BLOW TO THE HEAD, BUT I'VE JUST HAD AN IDEA FOR GETTING INSIDE THE PENITENTIARY...
I'VE HAD AN IDEA TOO, JOE!
I HAVEN'T, JOE...
LET'S COMPARE IDEAS! MINE IS THAT TO ENTER THE PENITENTIARY ...
...WE'D JUST HAVE TO DIG A TUNNEL...
...THAT WOULD START OUTSIDE THE WALLS AND LEAD INSIDE!
?
INCREDIBLE! WE HAD THE SAME IDEA! GENIUSES! WE'RE ALL GENIUSES!
EXCEPT FOR AVERELL.
YEAH, HE'S NOT EXACTLY BURDENED BY GENIUS!
BUT, JOE...
...THINK ABOUT IT! WE'RE USED TO DIGGING FROM THE INSIDE OUT! WHAT YOU'RE PROPOSING NOW IS AN ENTIRELY DIFFERENT TECHNIQUE, JOE!
HOW ABOUT A TASTE OF MY TRIED-AND-TRUE FIST-TO-NOSE TECHNIQUE, HUH?!!
35B

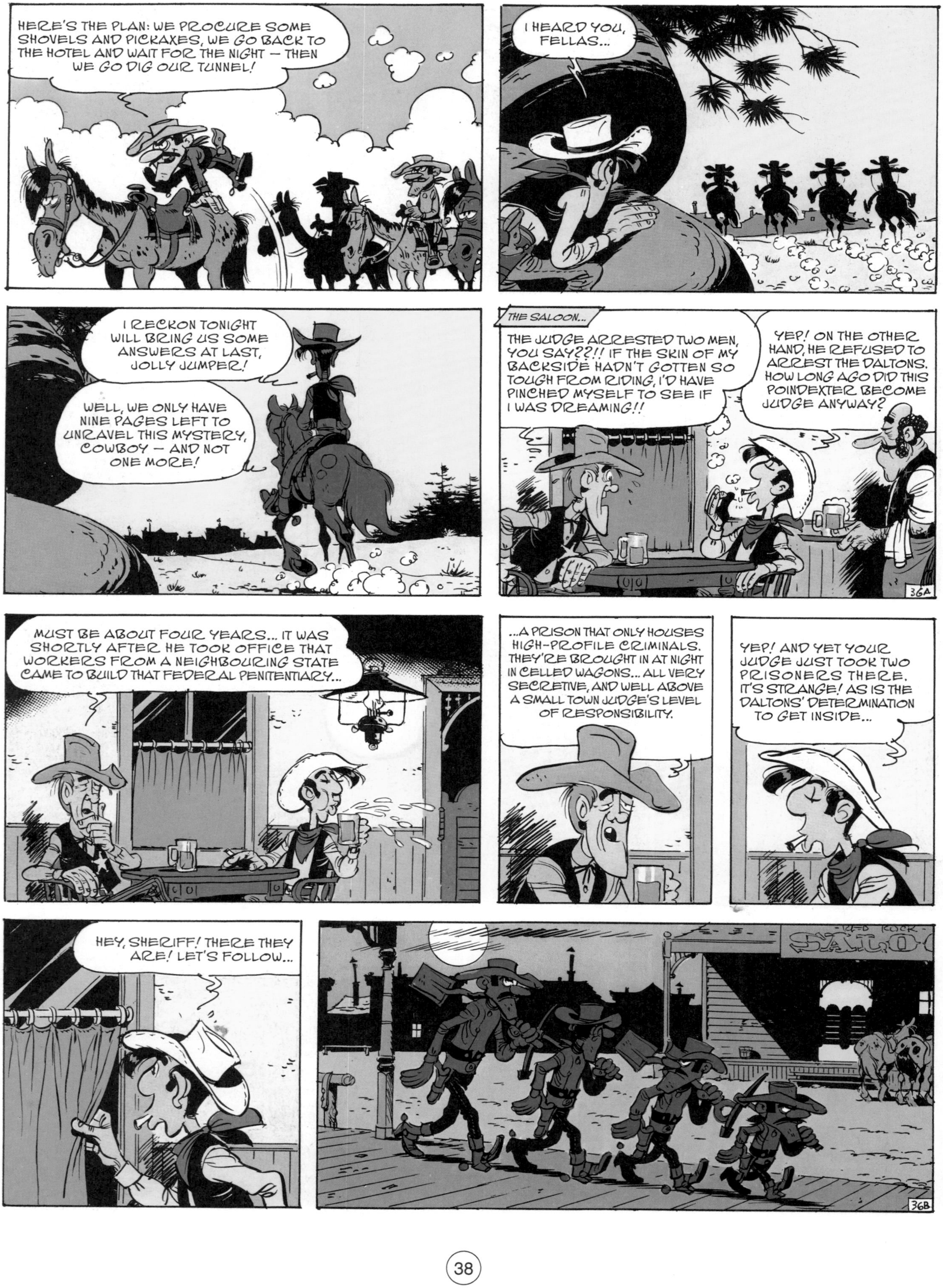
HERE'S THE PLAN: WE PROCURE SOME SHOVELS AND PICKAXES, WE GO BACK TO THE HOTEL AND WAIT FOR THE NIGHT — THEN WE GO DIG OUR TUNNEL!
I HEARD YOU, FELLAS...
I RECKON TONIGHT WILL BRING US SOME ANSWERS AT LAST, JOLLY JUMPER!
WELL, WE ONLY HAVE NINE PAGES LEFT TO UNRAVEL THIS MYSTERY, COWBOY — AND NOT ONE MORE!
THE SALOON...
THE JUDGE ARRESTED TWO MEN, YOU SAY??!! IF THE SKIN OF MY BACKSIDE HADN'T GOTTEN SO TOUGH FROM RIDING, I'D HAVE PINCHED MYSELF TO SEE IF I WAS DREAMING!!
YEP! ON THE OTHER HAND, HE REFUSED TO ARREST THE DALTONS. HOW LONG AGO DID THIS POINDEXTER BECOME JUDGE ANYWAY?
36A
MUST BE ABOUT FOUR YEARS... IT WAS SHORTLY AFTER HE TOOK OFFICE THAT WORKERS FROM A NEIGHBOURING STATE CAME TO BUILD THAT FEDERAL PENITENTIARY...
...A PRISON THAT ONLY HOUSES HIGH-PROFILE CRIMINALS. THEY'RE BROUGHT IN AT NIGHT IN CELLED WAGONS... ALL VERY SECRETIVE, AND WELL ABOVE A SMALL TOWN JUDGE'S LEVEL OF RESPONSIBILITY.
YEP! AND YET YOUR JUDGE JUST TOOK TWO PRISONERS THERE. IT'S STRANGE! AS IS THE DALTONS' DETERMINATION TO GET INSIDE...
HEY, SHERIFF! THERE THEY ARE! LET'S FOLLOW...
36B

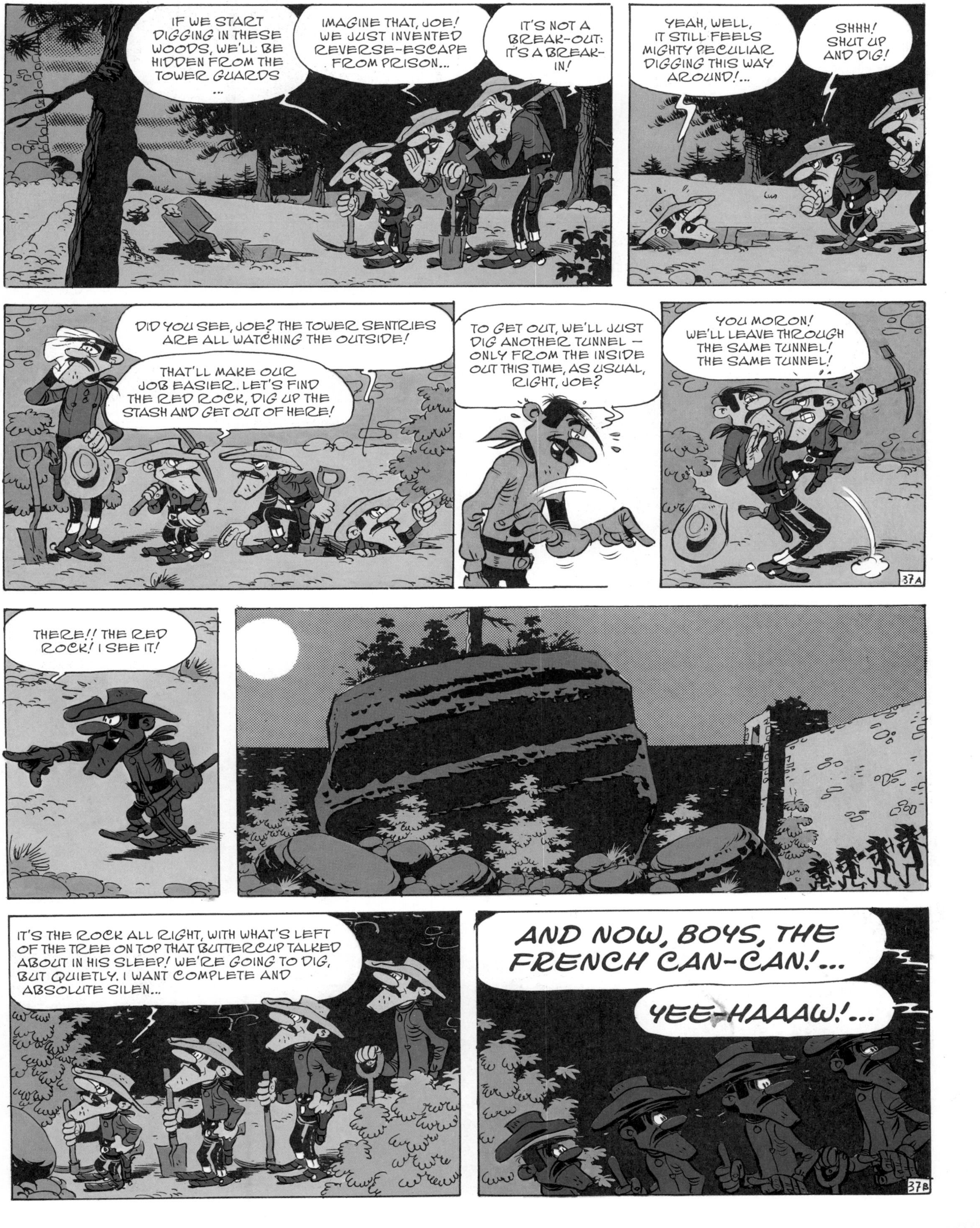
IF WE START DIGGING IN THESE WOODS, WE'LL BE HIDDEN FROM THE TOWER GUARDS ...
IMAGINE THAT, JOE! WE JUST INVENTED REVERSE-ESCAPE FROM PRISON...
IT'S NOT A BREAK-OUT: IT'S A BREAK-IN!
YEAH, WELL, IT STILL FEELS MIGHTY PECULIAR DIGGING THIS WAY AROUND!...
SHHH! SHUT UP AND DIG!
DID YOU SEE, JOE? THE TOWER SENTRIES ARE ALL WATCHING THE OUTSIDE!
THAT'LL MAKE OUR JOB EASIER.. LET'S FIND THE RED ROCK, DIG UP THE STASH AND GET OUT OF HERE!
TO GET OUT, WE'LL JUST DIG ANOTHER TUNNEL — ONLY FROM THE INSIDE OUT THIS TIME, AS USUAL, RIGHT, JOE?
YOU MORON! WE'LL LEAVE THROUGH THE SAME TUNNEL! THE SAME TUNNEL!
37A
THERE!! THE RED ROCK! I SEE IT!
IT'S THE ROCK ALL RIGHT, WITH WHAT'S LEFT OF THE TREE ON TOP THAT BUTTERCUP TALKED ABOUT IN HIS SLEEP! WE'RE GOING TO DIG, BUT QUIETLY. I WANT COMPLETE AND ABSOLUTE SILEN...
AND NOW, BOYS, THE FRENCH CAN-CAN!...
YEE-HAAAW!...
37B

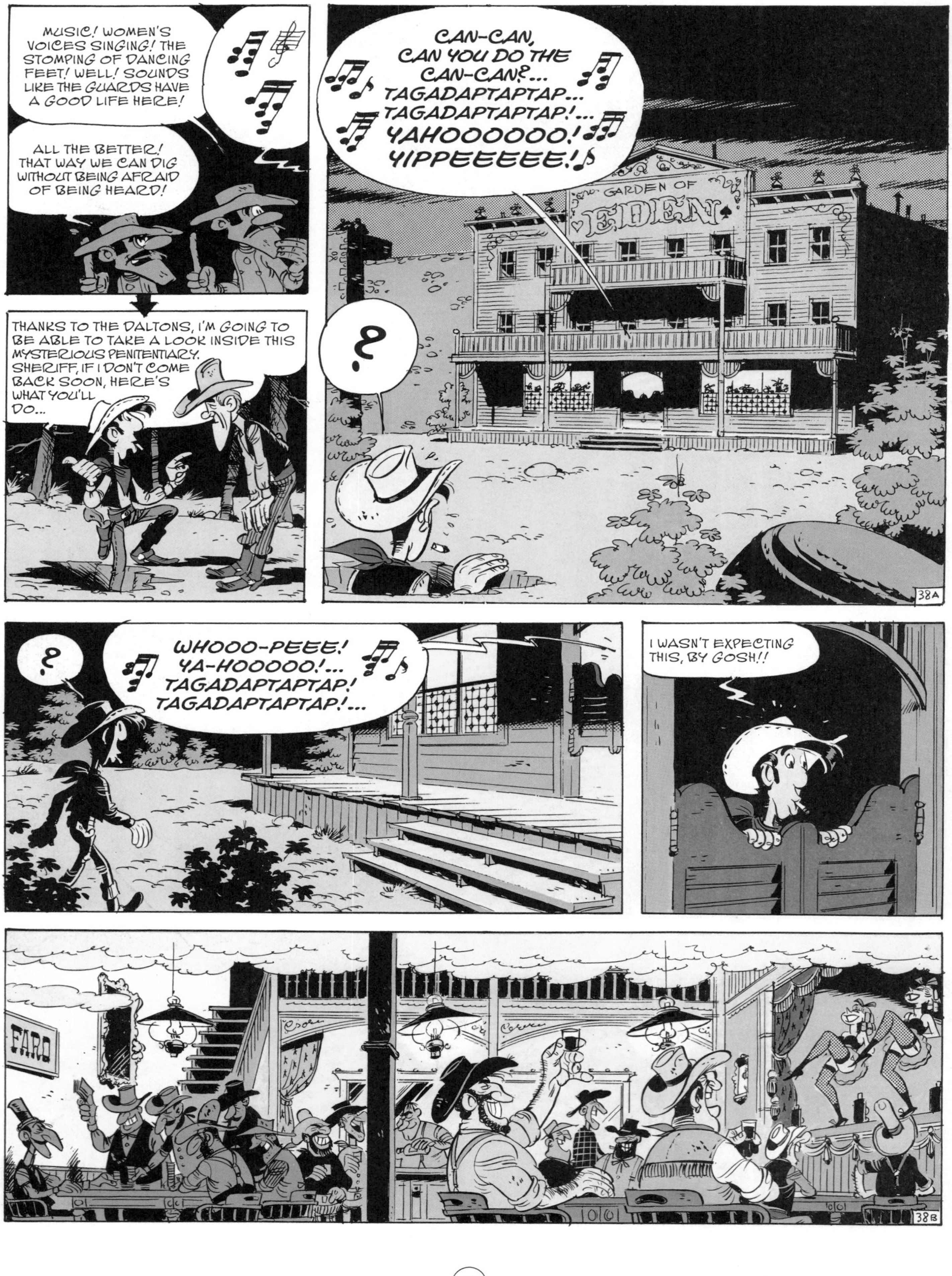
MUSIC! WOMEN'S VOICES SINGING! THE STOMPING OF DANCING FEET! WELL! SOUNDS LIKE THE GUARDS HAVE A GOOD LIFE HERE!
ALL THE BETTER! THAT WAY WE CAN DIG WITHOUT BEING AFRAID OF BEING HEARD!
THANKS TO THE DALTONS, I'M GOING TO BE ABLE TO TAKE A LOOK INSIDE THIS MYSTERIOUS PENITENTIARY. SHERIFF, IF I DON'T COME BACK SOON, HERE'S WHAT YOU'LL DO...
CAN-CAN, CAN YOU DO THE CAN-CAN?... TAGADAPTAPTAP... TAGADAPTAPTAP!... YAHOOOOOO! YIPPEEEEE!
GARDEN OF EDEN
?
38A
?
WHOOO-PEEE! YA-HOOOOO!... TAGADAPTAPTAP! TAGADAPTAPTAP!...
I WASN'T EXPECTING THIS, BY GOSH!!
FARO
38B

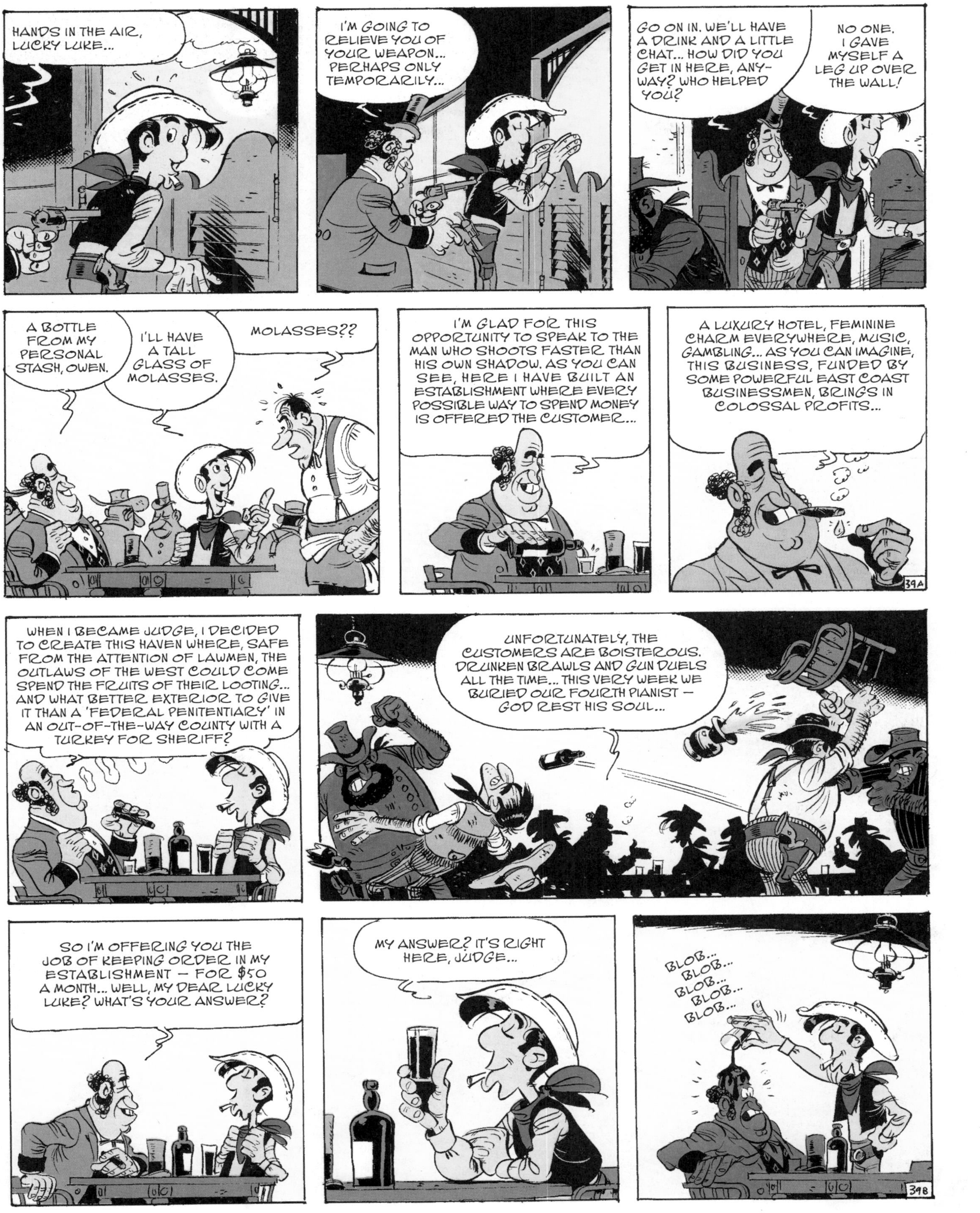
HANDS IN THE AIR, LUCKY LUKE...
I'M GOING TO RELIEVE YOU OF YOUR WEAPON... PERHAPS ONLY TEMPORARILY...
GO ON IN. WE'LL HAVE A DRINK AND A LITTLE CHAT... HOW DID YOU GET IN HERE, ANYWAY? WHO HELPED YOU?
NO ONE. I GAVE MYSELF A LEG UP OVER THE WALL!
A BOTTLE FROM MY PERSONAL STASH, OWEN.
I'LL HAVE A TALL GLASS OF MOLASSES.
MOLASSES??
I'M GLAD FOR THIS OPPORTUNITY TO SPEAK TO THE MAN WHO SHOOTS FASTER THAN HIS OWN SHADOW. AS YOU CAN SEE, HERE I HAVE BUILT AN ESTABLISHMENT WHERE EVERY POSSIBLE WAY TO SPEND MONEY IS OFFERED THE CUSTOMER...
A LUXURY HOTEL, FEMININE CHARM EVERYWHERE, MUSIC, GAMBLING... AS YOU CAN IMAGINE, THIS BUSINESS, FUNDED BY SOME POWERFUL EAST COAST BUSINESSMEN, BRINGS IN COLOSSAL PROFITS...
39A
WHEN I BECAME JUDGE, I DECIDED TO CREATE THIS HAVEN WHERE, SAFE FROM THE ATTENTION OF LAWMEN, THE OUTLAWS OF THE WEST COULD COME SPEND THE FRUITS OF THEIR LOOTING... AND WHAT BETTER EXTERIOR TO GIVE IT THAN A 'FEDERAL PENITENTIARY' IN AN OUT-OF-THE-WAY COUNTY WITH A TURKEY FOR SHERIFF?
UNFORTUNATELY, THE CUSTOMERS ARE BOISTEROUS. DRUNKEN BRAWLS AND GUN DUELS ALL THE TIME... THIS VERY WEEK WE BURIED OUR FOURTH PIANIST — GOD REST HIS SOUL...
SO I'M OFFERING YOU THE JOB OF KEEPING ORDER IN MY ESTABLISHMENT — FOR $50 A MONTH... WELL, MY DEAR LUCKY LUKE? WHAT'S YOUR ANSWER?
MY ANSWER? IT'S RIGHT HERE, JUDGE...
BLOB... BLOB... BLOB... BLOB... BLOB...
39B

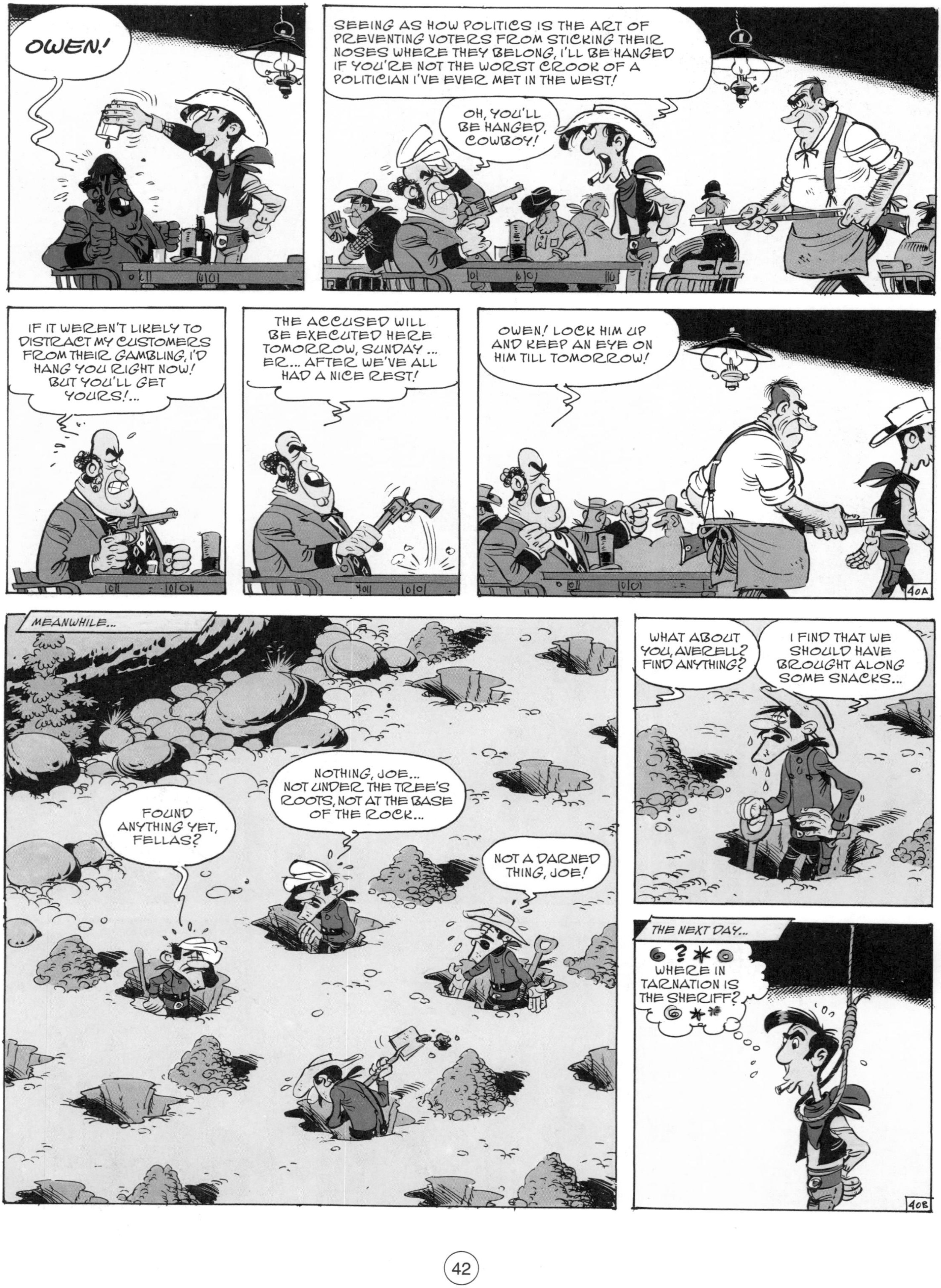

OWEN!
SEEING AS HOW POLITICS IS THE ART OF PREVENTING VOTERS FROM STICKING THEIR NOSES WHERE THEY BELONG, I'LL BE HANGED IF YOU'RE NOT THE WORST CROOK OF A POLITICIAN I'VE EVER MET IN THE WEST!
OH, YOU'LL BE HANGED, COWBOY!
IF IT WEREN'T LIKELY TO DISTRACT MY CUSTOMERS FROM THEIR GAMBLING, I'D HANG YOU RIGHT NOW! BUT YOU'LL GET YOURS!...
THE ACCUSED WILL BE EXECUTED HERE TOMORROW, SUNDAY ... ER... AFTER WE'VE ALL HAD A NICE REST!
OWEN! LOCK HIM UP AND KEEP AN EYE ON HIM TILL TOMORROW!
40A
MEANWHILE...
FOUND ANYTHING YET, FELLAS?
NOTHING, JOE... NOT UNDER THE TREE'S ROOTS, NOT AT THE BASE OF THE ROCK...
NOT A DARNED THING, JOE!
WHAT ABOUT YOU, AVERELL? FIND ANYTHING?
I FIND THAT WE SHOULD HAVE BROUGHT ALONG SOME SNACKS...
THE NEXT DAY...
WHERE IN TARNATION IS THE SHERIFF?
40B

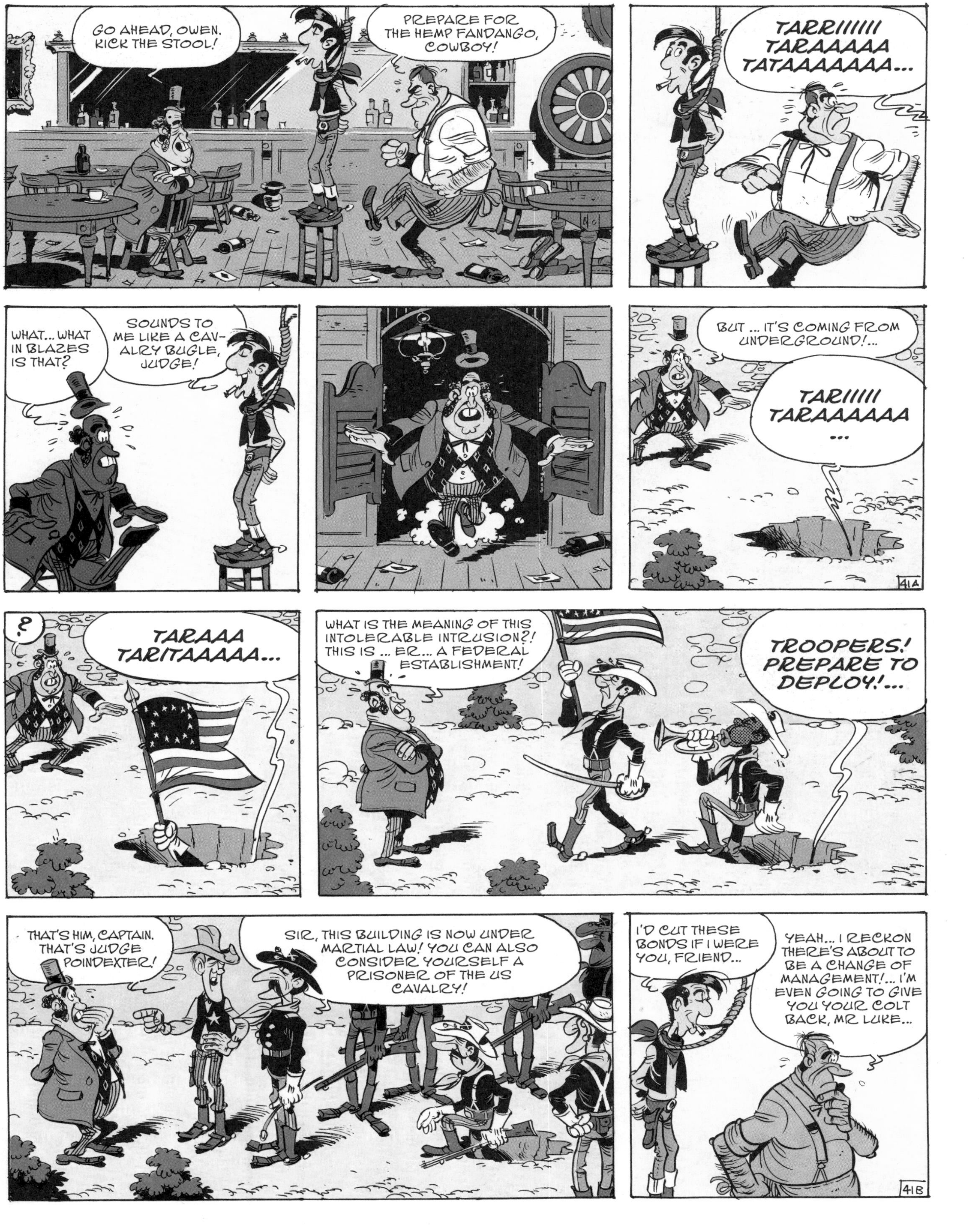

GO AHEAD, OWEN. KICK THE STOOL!
PREPARE FOR THE HEMP FANDANGO, COWBOY!
TARRIIIIII TARAAAAAA TATAAAAAAAA...
WHAT... WHAT IN BLAZES IS THAT?
SOUNDS TO ME LIKE A CAVALRY BUGLE, JUDGE!
BUT ... IT'S COMING FROM UNDERGROUND!...
TARIIIII TARAAAAAAA ...
41A
TARAAA TARITAAAAAA...
WHAT IS THE MEANING OF THIS INTOLERABLE INTRUSION?! THIS IS ... ER... A FEDERAL ESTABLISHMENT!
TROOPERS! PREPARE TO DEPLOY!...
THAT'S HIM, CAPTAIN. THAT'S JUDGE POINDEXTER!
SIR, THIS BUILDING IS NOW UNDER MARTIAL LAW! YOU CAN ALSO CONSIDER YOURSELF A PRISONER OF THE US CAVALRY!
I'D CUT THESE BONDS IF I WERE YOU, FRIEND...
YEAH... I RECKON THERE'S ABOUT TO BE A CHANGE OF MANAGEMENT!... I'M EVEN GOING TO GIVE YOU YOUR COLT BACK, MR LUKE...
41B

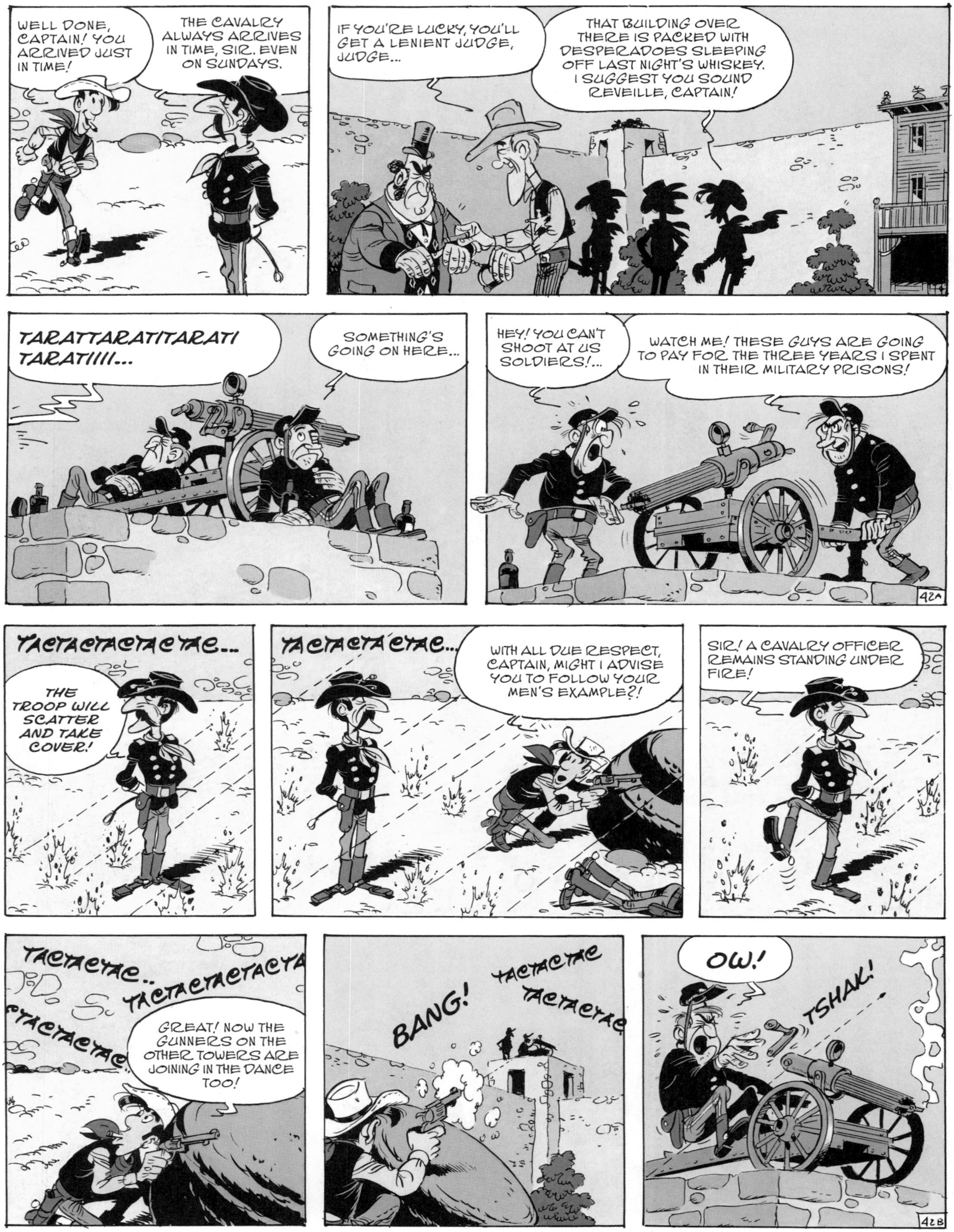
WELL DONE, CAPTAIN! YOU ARRIVED JUST IN TIME!
THE CAVALRY ALWAYS ARRIVES IN TIME, SIR. EVEN ON SUNDAYS.
IF YOU'RE LUCKY, YOU'LL GET A LENIENT JUDGE, JUDGE...
THAT BUILDING OVER THERE IS PACKED WITH DESPERADOES SLEEPING OFF LAST NIGHT'S WHISKEY. I SUGGEST YOU SOUND REVEILLE, CAPTAIN!
TARATTARATITARATI TARATIIIII...
SOMETHING'S GOING ON HERE...
HEY! YOU CAN'T SHOOT AT US SOLDIERS!...
WATCH ME! THESE GUYS ARE GOING TO PAY FOR THE THREE YEARS I SPENT IN THEIR MILITARY PRISONS!
42A
TACTACTACTACTAC TAC...
THE TROOP WILL SCATTER AND TAKE COVER!
TACTACTA CTAC...
WITH ALL DUE RESPECT, CAPTAIN, MIGHT I ADVISE YOU TO FOLLOW YOUR MEN'S EXAMPLE?!
SIR! A CAVALRY OFFICER REMAINS STANDING UNDER FIRE!
TACTACTAC..
TACTACTACTACTACTA
TACTACTAC
GREAT! NOW THE GUNNERS ON THE OTHER TOWERS ARE JOINING IN THE DANCE TOO!
BANG!
TACTACTAC
TACTACTAC
OW!
TSHAK!
42B

BANG!
OUCH!
TSHAK!
!
TSHUNK!
CLANG!
!
!
EXCELLENT SHOOTING, SIR!
YEP! IT'S THE FIRST TIME I'VE DISARMED OUTLAWS ARMED WITH MACHINE GUNS!
43A
BUGLER! SOUND THE CEASEFIRE!
TSK TSK TSK!...
PWAPWA PWETT PWWETT...
WHAT IS THE MEANING OF THIS MUSICAL IMPROVISATION, ARMSTRONG?
I'M AFRAID MY BUGLE WAS PIERCED SLIGHTLY BY A BULLET, CAPTAIN...
I KINDA LIKE THIS NEW SOUND, THOUGH...
THE LADIES AND THE PIANO PLAYER WILL LEAVE ON THE FIRST TRAIN. EVERYONE ELSE IS UNDER ARREST!
43B

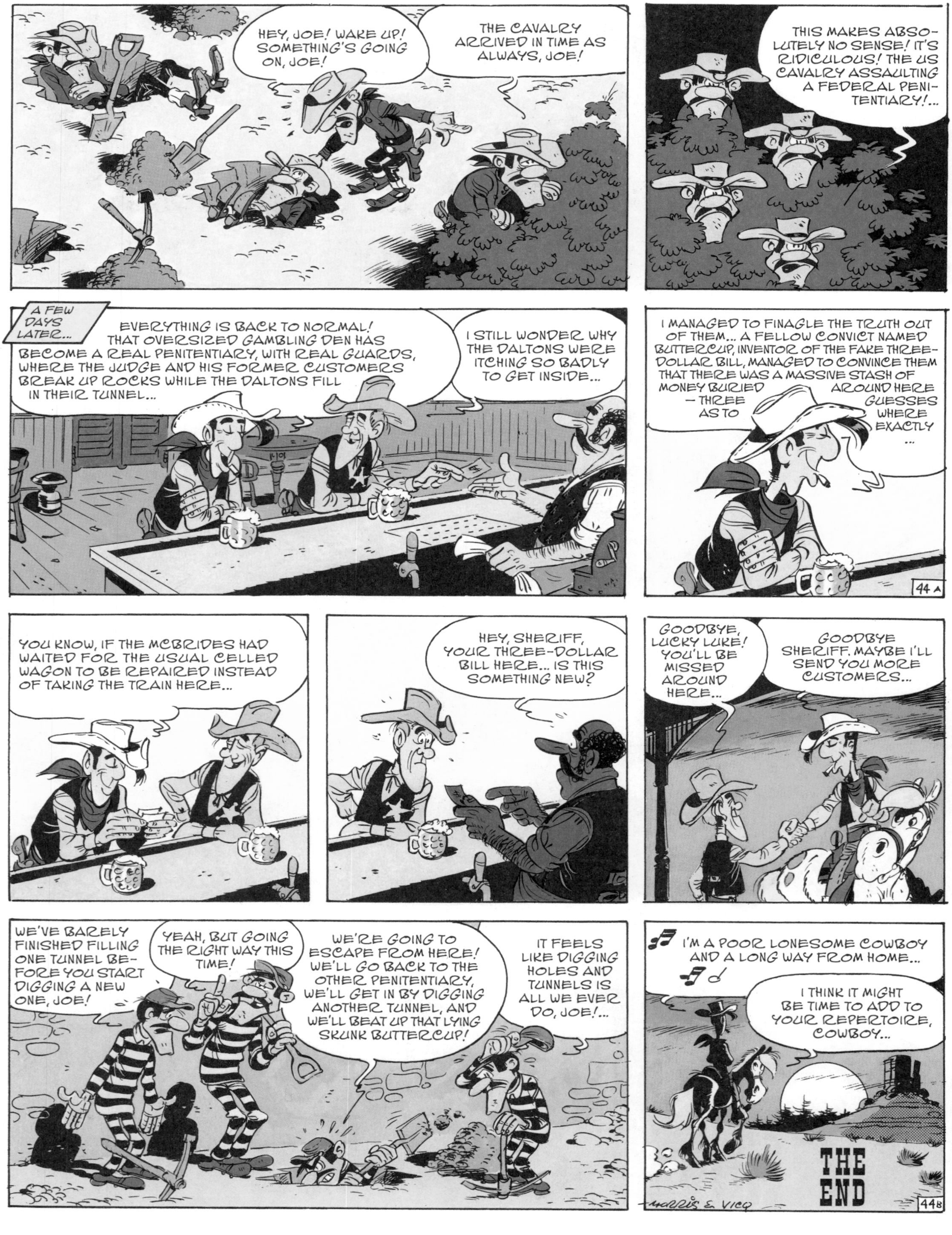
HEY, JOE! WAKE UP! SOMETHING'S GOING ON, JOE!
THE CAVALRY ARRIVED IN TIME AS ALWAYS, JOE!
THIS MAKES ABSOLUTELY NO SENSE! IT'S RIDICULOUS! THE US CAVALRY ASSAULTING A FEDERAL PENITENTIARY!...
A FEW DAYS LATER...
EVERYTHING IS BACK TO NORMAL! THAT OVERSIZED GAMBLING DEN HAS BECOME A REAL PENITENTIARY, WITH REAL GUARDS, WHERE THE JUDGE AND HIS FORMER CUSTOMERS BREAK UP ROCKS WHILE THE DALTONS FILL IN THEIR TUNNEL...
I STILL WONDER WHY THE DALTONS WERE ITCHING SO BADLY TO GET INSIDE...
I MANAGED TO FINAGLE THE TRUTH OUT OF THEM... A FELLOW CONVICT NAMED BUTTERCUP, INVENTOR OF THE FAKE THREE-DOLLAR BILL, MANAGED TO CONVINCE THEM THAT THERE WAS A MASSIVE STASH OF MONEY BURIED AROUND HERE – THREE GUESSES AS TO WHERE EXACTLY...
44 A
YOU KNOW, IF THE MCBRIDES HAD WAITED FOR THE USUAL CELLED WAGON TO BE REPAIRED INSTEAD OF TAKING THE TRAIN HERE...
HEY, SHERIFF, YOUR THREE-DOLLAR BILL HERE... IS THIS SOMETHING NEW?
GOODBYE, LUCKY LUKE! YOU'LL BE MISSED AROUND HERE...
GOODBYE SHERIFF. MAYBE I'LL SEND YOU MORE CUSTOMERS...
WE'VE BARELY FINISHED FILLING ONE TUNNEL BEFORE YOU START DIGGING A NEW ONE, JOE!
YEAH, BUT GOING THE RIGHT WAY THIS TIME!
WE'RE GOING TO ESCAPE FROM HERE! WE'LL GO BACK TO THE OTHER PENITENTIARY, WE'LL GET IN BY DIGGING ANOTHER TUNNEL, AND WE'LL BEAT UP THAT LYING SKUNK BUTTERCUP!
IT FEELS LIKE DIGGING HOLES AND TUNNELS IS ALL WE EVER DO, JOE!...
I'M A POOR LONESOME COWBOY AND A LONG WAY FROM HOME...
I THINK IT MIGHT BE TIME TO ADD TO YOUR REPERTOIRE, COWBOY...
THE END
MORRIS & VICQ
44B

presents

LUCKY LUKE

The man who shoots faster than his own shadow

COMING SOON

JUNE 2016

AUGUST 2016

OCTOBER 2016

DECEMBER 2016